Totally Bound Publishing books by Maggie Mitchell:

Muses Across Time Volume One
Chasing Terpsichore
Calling Calliope

I0628148

MUSES ACROSS TIME
Volume One

Chasing Terpsichore

Calling Calliope

MAGGIE MITCHELL

Muses Across Time Volume One
ISBN # 978-1-78430-181-1
©Copyright Maggie Mitchell 2014
Cover Art by Posh Gosh ©Copyright 2014
Interior text design by Claire Siemaszkiewicz
Totally Bound Publishing

Published in 2014 by Totally Bound Publishing, Newland House, The Point, Weaver Road, Lincoln, LN6 3QN, United Kingdom.

CHASING
TERPSICHORE

Dedication

For everyone who helped me keep faith in this one. I
love you all. You know who you are!

Chapter One

Sydney, Australia
Present day

A shrouded figure stood alone in a secluded corner of the club. He scanned the area, looking from one side of the smoke-filled room to the other.

These mortals disgust me with their decadence, but perhaps they shall serve their purpose and assist me with my revenge.

A lone dancer stood upon a high platform, encased in a cage to prevent human contact. He watched in fascination as she danced, oblivious to his or anyone else's presence. She moved with grace and elegance, her body the epitome of feminine perfection. She rubbed her hips against the cold metal surface, then wrapped her muscular leg around the central pole supporting her while she arched her back. She thrust her firm breasts high while she sighed with the pleasure of letting her inhibitions go. It was almost a shame to destroy all that beauty, but he couldn't allow himself to feel guilt for taking her life away from her.

After what Zeus had put him through, he would not rest until he had his revenge. He would make her suffering great, and thus punish Zeus in the most effective way possible—through his children.

His precious daughters will forever be trapped in the Underworld and I will have my revenge on the one who destroyed my life.

* * * *

Oh, it feels so good!

It never failed to move her. The thrill she experienced every time she danced here at The Cave, Sydney's premier dance club. She didn't do it very often, but she loved it. It was the closest Corey got to the feeling of being home at Pieria, near Mount Olympus. Who would have thought that Terpsichore, the Muse of Dance, would be pole dancing in a fancy discotheque in Sydney? Certainly not Corey herself, although she had wished for the power to travel to other dimensions—little had she known that one day she would be doing just that. Except she had no idea how Hera had sent her here, or, more to the point, how to get home.

Oh the irony. Once she'd looked down on those who served her but now she was one of the ones who served. Wouldn't her family be shocked to know she worked for money, and, worse than that, she was a tango teaching pole dancer!

She giggled as she pictured the scene in her father's court. Zeus had a pretty strong opinion on manual labor and working for payment—especially his progeny. Gods and goddesses should be served, not the other way around. He'd probably lock her up for a month if he found out — or worse. *If I ever find my way back home to Olympus, that is.*

No point in worrying about that right now, she thought as she took another ankle spin around the pole. She jumped when someone's hand reached up from below her platform and grabbed her ankle through the bars of the cage. She scanned the crowd and found the culprit. A randy, twenty-something guy with a stupid grin was attempting to slide his palm higher up her calf.

Oh no you don't!

She lifted her foot in an attempt to shake him off, but he dug in his fingers and gripped harder. *Great. Just great.* Even though The Cave was more of a retro sixties club, occasionally some overenthusiastic patron hoped for a bit more of a show — just her luck to have one of those idiots zero in on her tonight. Her irritation increased when her second attempt to dislodge him failed and his sweaty skin sent shivers of revulsion through her. A pounding started inside her head and her eyes flashed fire and light, aiming directly at her captive's offending body part

Holy crap. Did she just send a fireball at that boy? Her powers must finally be coming back.

Yay!

But this probably wasn't the time to rejoice because she prayed to the gods that she hadn't hurt him. Annoying thing that he was, he was still an innocent mortal. Even as she'd thought it, she marveled at how she'd changed. Back home she wouldn't have given it a second thought.

Amazing what living with mortals can do for you.

The young man released her leg instantly, as he fell down to the floor below. "Ow! What the f—?" He waved his hand back and forth, blowing on his fingers before dunking them in his glass of beer.

"She burned me, the bitch!"

One of his mates laughed and slapped him on the back. "How could she burn you, dude? All you did was touch her leg. She didn't even move."

He pulled his hand out of the glass and inspected it. Corey leaned over the cage to get a look. Nothing. No marks, no blisters, no redness and now, apparently, no pain.

"Shit, this is just too weird," said the boy. "Let's get the hell out of here. I've had enough of this place."

Relieved to find that she hadn't accidentally caused the boy harm, Corey watched the group leave and sighed. She'd either have to give up the pole-dancing gig, or have her cage elevated higher. She loved being at The Cave but she'd only agreed to dance here if she could be out of reach of the patrons. As much as she enjoyed the dancing, she didn't want to be so close to the audience. Having strangers try to touch her wasn't something she was willing to put up with. She shuddered to think of what might have happened if that incident had happened at home. If that young man had even touched her with a whisker in her homeland, her father would have executed him for daring to lay a finger on one of his offspring.

She hadn't meant the young man any harm, but she hadn't known her powers would decide to come back at that moment. Normally the mortal Corey wouldn't have lost her temper, but she'd had a particularly crappy day so far. Her students had been extra trying and today would probably set a new world record for having her foot stamped on.

However, when she thought about it, of all the things she missed about home, she didn't miss the brutal consequences. In fact life here among the mortals in Australia was actually pretty darn good. She danced away her days teaching at Terpsichore's Tango school, and a couple of nights a month she indulged herself with pole dancing at The Cave.

Of course, her friends didn't know about her real identity. She wasn't stupid. They'd lock her away if she ever mentioned it. Not for one minute would they believe that she was Terpsichore, the Muse of Dance, goddess, and daughter of Zeus. Heck, from what she'd learned about society here in Sydney, she wouldn't believe her either. To them she was just Corey, a dance teacher, and that's the way she wanted it to stay. Apart from her penchant for having fun, she was through with being the center of attention, so being a slightly quirky dance teacher who was accepted at face value was just fine with her.

She stopped dancing, giggling to herself as she thought about it. It was probably true her friends thought of her as more than just a tad eccentric. More to the point, they probably thought she was a lot eccentric. She shrugged. It didn't really matter anymore. Here she could get away with it. So what if her clothes always made a fashion statement and she liked to have fun as often as she could? Did it matter that she thought sleeping was overrated? She didn't know how long she was going to be here so there was little time to get bogged down with seriousness when there was some fun to be had.

But it wasn't all about the fun. There was something else about her that her friends didn't know. This was probably the most surprising change she'd made since she'd arrived in this time. She'd started teaching underprivileged kids from the community center and for the first time in her life she knew the joy of doing something for others and not expecting anything back. Who knew? She actually felt pretty darn good about it and if that made her eccentric, then so be it.

Her sister Calliope was always saying one never knew what was around the corner, and Corey was living proof of that. One minute she had been at home with her family and *poof*, she was trapped here in another time, another place and another dimension.

Hera had a lot to answer for, but Corey had to admit that she'd learned a lot about herself since she'd been here. When and if she did return home, her family would find her changed, and she sure as heck was going to show them just how much she'd missed them.

After unlocking her cage from the inside, Corey threw out the rope ladder and climbed down to the back of the platform. Her lungs closed in on her from the smoke haze as she reached the bottom rung. She'd had enough for tonight. Using her powers on that kid had surprised the heck out of her. She'd forgotten what it felt like and she wasn't sure she even liked it now. At least he didn't seem to be any worse for the experience. It was a solid reminder to her that she really needed to be less conspicuous. Being a goddess meant she had a perfect body shape that many men liked looking at and women seemed to envy. From now on she'd have to tone down her looks, especially if her powers were coming back. She didn't need another accidental zap happening. Her powers did seem a bit rusty and she needed to take things slowly while she figured out how she could use them to get back home.

She snuck out of the back door and made her way down the dark alley toward her car. She rested her body against the wall in the lane way, and leaned forward to take off her high heels so she could rub her aching feet. The sound of a police siren startled her as she slipped the shoes back on and peered out of the alleyway to see what was happening at the front of the club.

Oh crap, it's a raid. So much for staying inconspicuous.

Ducking back into the alley she prayed to the gods that the police hadn't seen her. All she wanted to do was go home. When the ruckus calmed down, she decided to take her chances and stepped outside. When she was almost to the end of the block and in sight of her car, she breathed a sigh of relief.

She felt a hand on her shoulder, scaring the bejeezus out of her.

She turned her head to find a cop stopping her from moving, accompanied by that kid from the bar.

"That's her, officer. She's the one," said the kid, smirking at her as he took a step forward.

She opened her mouth as the surprise set in. "What the heck are you talking about?"

The cop looked from the young man to Corey, taking his time, his eyes moving up and down her smutty attire.

Oh great. The one time I don't take the time to change into my street clothes and this happens. "Look, officer, I can explain—"

The kid grabbed onto the cop's arm. "Who are you going to believe, the word of a hooker or the son of a prominent judge?"

This kid was beginning to annoy her big time.

The cop lifted his eyebrows and sighed. "I'm sorry, miss, but soliciting a minor is an offense. I'll have to take you in and charge you."

"What? I didn't solicit anyone. I was only dancing. I didn't even speak to him—hang on, did you say minor? Then what was he doing in The Cave in the first place?"

The kid smirked again. She was really beginning to dislike this spoiled brat.

"I wasn't in any club," he said, poking his tongue out at her while the cop wasn't looking. "You propositioned me here in the alley, bitch!"

The policeman stepped between the two of them as Corey tried to move closer to her accuser. As she restrained herself from an overwhelming urge to zap him again, the boy must have picked up on her train of thought and retreated. "Careful, officer," he said as he stepped backwards. "She burns."

"That's enough, kid," said the cop as he placed a small notebook in his shirt pocket. "I have your details, now move on. Show's over. I'll take it from here." The cop took her arm, gesturing for her to place her hands behind her back before he attached plastic restraints to her wrists. He then ushered her toward a police car that conveniently waited on the corner, pushing her into the back seat with his hand firmly on her head.

Oh my goddess, they really do that. Just like in the movies.

Shuffling forward in the seat as well as she could with her hands tied, she leaned toward the front seat where the cop was now sitting. "Officer, you can't arrest me. I didn't do anything except dance."

The cop started the car and angled his head to check his mirrors. "You'll get your chance to talk when we get to the station," he said as he put the car into gear and drove away from the curb. "In the meantime, keep your trap shut. I've got a real humdinger of a headache and I get really nasty when I don't get my peace and quiet."

"Am I really under arrest then?"

At the corner of the lane as the car slowed to a stop, the cop turned his head and nodded toward her cuffed hands. "Well, duh."

She twisted her wrists back and forth under the cuffs. "But you didn't read me my rights."

"You watch too much television, woman. This isn't the US of A. It's Sydney, Australia, and we don't have any of those fancy Miranda rights here, but if it makes you any happier, you're under arrest, and anything you say may be used against you, so shut the hell up."

Oh lucky me. A surly comedian. This just gets better and better.

* * * *

James Barrington straightened his red silk tie and smoothed the collar of his white shirt while his secretary, Susan, asked him for her first legal advice favor in the entire three years she'd worked for him. "You want me to represent who?"

Susan held out his suit jacket for him, sleeves open, so he could slip his arms right into it. "My dance teacher, Corey. There's been a bit of a misunderstanding."

"Your dance teacher? You mean the tango teacher?" She nodded as he pulled the edges of the suit down to straighten the line. "What sort of misunderstanding?" Retrieving his comb from his pocket, he lifted his hand to tidy up his never-a-strand-out-of-place blond hair.

"She's been arrested for prostitution," said Susan as she closed the closet door.

The comb dropped to the floor.

He turned back to face her. "For a minute there I thought you said prostitution?"

"I did," she said as she bent down, picked up the comb and handed it back to him. "However, she isn't a prostitute. It's all a horrible mistake," she said. "You have to help her sort out this mess."

He sighed. "Susan, you know I only do corporate law now. It's been years since I worked a criminal case. I can give you a number of recommendations for criminal law specialists."

"No, I don't want anyone else. I don't trust anyone else, James. Corey has no one and you're the best solicitor I know. Come on, it won't take long to get it sorted." She looked at him with her little girl, butter wouldn't melt in her mouth, pleading face that he could never resist. "Please?"

James lifted a pile of files off the desk and placed them inside his brown leather satchel, before he moved to the door and turned around to face her.

"I have a meeting with Henderson in an hour. I won't have time to do anything until this afternoon," he lifted his wrist to check his watch. "If at all today."

Susan turned away quickly, her cheeks turning a deep shade of pink. "Um, ah..." she stuttered. "I rescheduled it for tomorrow."

James tried to hide the twitching of his lips. She thought she was a master manipulator when it came to getting him to do things he didn't want to do in the office. This was slightly different as she'd never asked him to represent anyone before, but he found her clumsy attempts amusing. He'd left criminal law behind when he'd chosen to follow in his father's footsteps, but he did owe Susan a favor, considering all the extra hours she'd put in lately. And she never complained. He walked back to his desk and dropped the satchel. He might as well surrender now and save himself the trouble of dealing with a pouting secretary. "All right then. Tell me the rest."

It was almost worth it just to see Susan's face light up. She was a nice-looking girl, but when she smiled, she was almost beautiful. Now he knew what his junior partner, Thomas, saw in her. Susan and Thomas had been dating for the last few weeks and James couldn't be happier. The pressure was off him, now that Susan was over her crush on him.

"Well, it all started when this boy grabbed her leg while she was pole dancing at King's Cross."

"You're kidding, right?"

* * * *

"You're kidding, right?"

Susan shook her head and whispered across the table. "Now why would I kid you? James is a really good solicitor. Why don't you want him to help you?"

Corey looked across the room at the six foot tall hunk of conservative male skulking near the door. It was obvious that he didn't want to be here. Susan must have told some fantastic story to drag her boss all the way up here to King's Cross to help a stranger. But she didn't want a solicitor who didn't want to be here. She leaned over the table and whispered back, "He doesn't want to help me. I can tell he's just here because you asked him." She nodded toward James as he spoke in hushed tones with a police officer at the door. "I really appreciate it, Susan, but I need a solicitor who has his heart in it. He doesn't even want to be in the same room with me. Give him a break. He probably has no idea what to do for a criminal case."

The lanky solicitor spun around to face them, his voice cold. "I'll have you know I've represented dozens of criminal cases in the past. I might practice a different type of law now, but that is by choice, not aptitude."

Corey threw her hands up in the air. "My point exactly. He doesn't want to do it, Susan. Give me another name."

James stiffened his back, and judging by the way he was shooting some proverbial smoke out of his ears, he wanted this less than she did. "I am perfectly capable of handling your case, Miss—"

Corey looked at him properly for the first time. Wow, what a cutie. Susan had never mentioned that her boss was so gorgeous—an uptight bastard, but gorgeous all the same. She caught a very manly, citrusy scent that must be his aftershave, and those blue eyes flashing at her really were magnificent. "It's Miss Olympia, but you can call me Corey," she said, as she flipped a stray curl off her forehead. "Now, James... I can call you James, can't I?"

His eyes widened a little, showing just a small chink in his strong facade of control. "Fine."

She smiled brightly, summoning all of her charm. "Good, that's much more friendly." Now that she had his attention, she lowered her voice, aiming for just that hint of huskiness she knew most men couldn't resist. "James, I don't want you to do this for me unless you believe in me."

The edge of his mouth twitched, betraying the barest hint of humor under that stiff composure. "Susan believes in you, Miss Olympia, and I have a lot of respect for her judgment. I agreed to help you and I intend to keep my word."

Her heart rate ramped up as she realized she really wanted it to be him. "Wonderful. Your overwhelming enthusiasm is appreciated." She winked at her friend Susan, whose lips trembled as she valiantly tried not to laugh. "I suppose I'd better tell you the whole story then."

Corey picked up her glass of water from the table and took a sip before starting. "I didn't do anything wrong except stop a randy teenager from pawing me." She wiped her hand over her mouth to wipe up the excess moisture and looked up into cool blue eyes. "How would I know his father is a prominent judge?"

"Judge?" James turned to Susan, who had slumped back in her chair with her head down. "Susan," he snapped. "You didn't mention anything about a judge?"

Corey stood up and moved behind Susan, placing her hand on her friend's shoulder. "Don't blame her — she didn't know the full story. I forgot to mention that bit."

"A fairly significant part you forgot to mention. If you want my help, Corey, you had better start from the beginning." He dragged her chair farther out from under the table and ushered her into it before placing his satchel on the floor and pulling out a legal pad and pencil.

Corey focused on his hands as he started writing. He had beautiful hands with long, perfectly shaped fingers and neat, short nails. If not for the interesting calluses she would have called them feminine. But feminine he definitely wasn't. *Hmm... So he doesn't spend all of his time in an office.* Those hands brought to mind all sorts of things he could do to her body and she sighed.

"Corey?" James stopped writing and started drumming his fingers on the table.

"Huh?" *Oops. Caught napping again. I'd better pay attention.* "Oh, yes. Well, I dance in a high cage so no one can get to me, but this idiot kid decided he wanted to grab my leg. When I shook him off, I guess he must have been disappointed."

"So how exactly did you shake him off?"

How could she put this so that it sounded plausible? She couldn't tell him she had zapped the kid with a fire bolt. "Umm… I shook my leg until he let go?"

Picking up the arrest report, James read a few lines before lifting his eyes. "He says in his statement he wasn't even in the club. He states you called him over to the alleyway, propositioned him, and when he declined, you burned his hand with a cigarette."

Corey stood up, shoving her chair away from the table, the legs of the chair screeching across the dirty linoleum floor, and placed her hands face down on the scratched surface. "I did no such thing! If he has a cigarette burn, he must have done it himself."

James arched his brow. "So your story is that he grabbed your leg, you shook him off, he let go, then left the club. Is that it?"

She walked across to the window and crossed her arms around her middle as she stared out into the courtyard below. "It's not a story, James. That's what happened. I never spoke to him in the alleyway. I am not a prostitute, I'm a dance teacher. Period. That rat is just trying to cover his butt for getting caught underage in a club."

James flipped a page on the police report and looked up again. "He says a bouncer from your club lured him into the alley from MacLeay Street. His father is threatening to sue The Cave for corrupting a minor."

He stood up and joined Corey at the window, close enough for her to smell his expensive aftershave.

This situation was getting weirder by the minute. Some snotty-nosed kid with a god complex was trying to ruin her life because he hadn't gotten his own way. Sounded like the sort of stuff she and her sisters used to do back home on Olympus—even resorting to using his father to help him get out of trouble.

Oh crap. Have I been as bad as this kid? Is this some sort of warped poetic justice for past misdeeds?

James placed his hand on her shoulder in a surprisingly comforting gesture. "I know this kid's father. I'll go speak to him and see if we can get this sorted out."

* * * *

James closed the door to the office of Judge Whittaker and smiled. He couldn't believe how easy it had been. One mention of the interesting story it made, having the son of an upstanding judge caught in a King's Cross exotic dancers' nightclub. It wasn't quite as bad as a strip club, but it came pretty close. The media would ignore the subtle differences and the general public certainly didn't care.

The gentleman's old boys' network did come in handy sometimes, with James' father the golf partner of the judge. It was one of the first things he learned about the law. Ninety percent of cases were won or lost in the clubs, the restaurants and the offices of solicitors, barristers and judges. Not exactly truth, justice and equality for the downtrodden, but sometimes one had to work the system to get what one wanted.

And he had what he wanted now. With this stupid, annoying case over, he could relax. By the time he had returned to the police station, the call from the judge should have been received, letting the crazy Miss Olympia off the hook. How his sensible, intelligent and usually conservative secretary had hooked up with that woman he'd never know.

She dressed like a slut and danced around a pole in a club at King's Cross in her spare time. *She teaches the tango. Enough said.*

However, he couldn't help but smile when he thought about her. She definitely had vitality. He wondered what she looked like under that wig and makeup. Her eyes were magnificent, that deep sea-green color so vibrant it had to be colored contacts. No one had eyes that color naturally. They reminded him of the aquamarine waters of the Aegean. He'd traveled there during his gap year after school and he hadn't thought about that trip to the Greek Islands for quite some time. One day soon, he'd have to make time to go back. Once he'd established himself as Queen's Counsel. If he ever had time off again.

As he hailed a cab from outside the Supreme Court, he sighed, reminding himself of the many briefs on his desk and how there were too many pending cases for him to be distracted by this case, or this woman — or holidays in exotic locations. Since the recent rise in high-profile CEOs getting caught with their hands in the till, it was a busy time for corporate law barristers. No time to think about idyllic beaches or sparkling green eyes. Besides, no one could be further away from his 'type' than her. She made him smile when she batted those amazing eyes at him, but that wasn't a bad thing, was it? Come to think of it, her eyes were not the only part of her that made him smile. There was…that outfit. *Oh yeah.* That skimpy tank top had barely covered her chest, and what purpose did that scrap of material around her middle fulfill? A skirt? It certainly showed off her legs. And those glorious legs went on forever.

Good God man, snap out of it.

He spent the short taxi ride back to the police station annoyed at his lack of control. Instead, he should keep his eye on his job. The law was predictable, and with it, he knew where he stood. He didn't have time to think about any woman, let alone a crazy, pole-dancing tango teacher. Hell, he had a career to think about. The promise he'd made to his father weighed on his mind, but he *would* follow in his father's footsteps and become a Queen's Counsel. Even though the idea didn't exactly set him on fire, he wasn't about to change his mind and disappoint his father. To get where he needed to be, he needed order in his life and Miss Corey Olympia represented total chaos. The sooner he wrapped this case up, the better.

But she still made him smile and she certainly was gorgeous. He chuckled as he anticipated this one last time to let her flirt with him. After today, he could move on and forget all about her. So why did he have trouble convincing himself it would be easy?

When the desk sergeant told him she'd already been released, he should have been relieved. Instead, he felt the disappointment sorely as he took a cab back to his apartment where a boring evening filled with paperwork awaited.

* * * *

The doorbell rang around eleven o'clock as James shut down his laptop, about to turn in. *Who the hell is visiting at this time of night?*

Peering through his peephole, he saw a woman. A woman he didn't recognize. A gorgeous woman he didn't recognize, who pressed his doorbell quite insistently.

"Okay, okay, I'm coming."

He opened the door and the woman flung herself at him, throwing her arms around his neck and kissing him smack bang on the mouth. Not just any old kiss either. *Holy crap.* Sparks flew from the first fiery touch of her soft, but demanding mouth on his.

Who is this woman?

Then again, his hormones said something else—*who cares?*

The softness of her lips belied the intoxicating power of her taste, mixed with the heady scent of her skin. His senses were overloaded as the woman snaked her fingers into his hair and she drew nearer to his body, pressing her breasts so close he could feel the outline of her taut nipples.

Somehow reality kicked in. *What in God's name am I doing kissing a strange woman?* Reluctantly he withdrew, placing his hands on her shoulders to steady her as he pushed her away, his breathing as rapid as a freight train. "Okay, you have my attention now." She opened her eyes and looked up into his face.

Aquamarine eyes, the color of the Aegean. *No, it can't be.*

Afraid he knew the answer already, he asked anyway. "Care to tell me who you are and what you're doing here?"

She smiled. "Don't you recognize me, James?" Pouting, she placed her hand dramatically over her chest. "I'm deeply wounded."

He laughed. Somehow he thought her ego could take it. She looked more like the cat who had swallowed the cream than a wounded one. Still, he couldn't believe this beautiful woman before him was the self-same, pole-dancing tango teacher he'd met that afternoon. She definitely cleaned up well, and his tightening pants could certainly attest to that. "Miss Olympia? I didn't recognize you. You look different."

Picking up his hand, she turned it over before tracing his heart line with her index finger. "It's Corey, and aren't you going to invite me in?"

He stood back to let her through. "Sure, come in." Warning bells rang loudly in his head, but he ignored them as she sauntered past him, her hips swaying seductively as she made her way to his couch. *What does she want?* He'd already decided she wasn't his type, although she did look better in her surprisingly conservative clothes. With her high–collared white shirt buttoned all the way up to the top and a colorful skirt swishing and swirling around her ankles, no skin showed at all. Yet she still managed to look enticingly sexy. The biggest surprise was her hair. He'd known the blonde mop was a wig, but he never would have guessed at the crowning glory under it. Her hair was magnificent with those amazing red curls flowing way past her shoulders. His hands itched to touch it and feel the softness between his fingers.

Jeez, he needed to get a grip.

"Nice place you have here, James." she said. She smiled while making herself at home on his couch, spreading her arms languorously over the top of it.

He stared at the gorgeous body sitting on his couch. She confounded him and he asked himself again — *Why is she here?* "Is there a problem with the charges? The judge dropped them, didn't he?"

"No problems at all. In fact, that's why I'm here. To thank you." Her green eyes twinkled. "I'd be in real trouble if not for your help. I am deeply in your debt."

Remembering the heat of that kiss, he shifted from one foot to another. "Consider me thanked."

She lifted her eyebrows and smiled again, a cute little dimple appearing on her cheek. "Oh no, James. I am nowhere near finished thanking you yet."

His trousers tightened painfully at her cheeky words. *Holy shit.* How did this woman get him so revved up inside?

She stood up and glided over to him, picked up his hand and proceeded to drag him toward the couch, sending tingles through his arm and all over his whole body.

"I disagree," he said, his voice sounding much huskier than he wanted it to.

She sat back down again and he fell onto the couch with her, landing so close that he braced his free hand on the wall behind to stop himself from falling on top of her. She smiled, winking at him as he struggled to put some extra space between them. "No, really…"

Using her fingers, she kneaded gently along his arm and stopped when she reached his shoulder. "Now don't go all stuffy on me, James. I know how you kiss, and you kiss darn well, so you can't fool me."

He coughed to clear his throat and attempted to stand. "Really, there is no need to thank me," he said in a voice that sounded at least two octaves higher than usual. "Can I get you something to drink?" *Smooth, James, real smooth.*

She increased the pressure of her hand on his shoulder, surprising him with her strength and stopping him from moving. "You can relax, James. I'm not going to jump on you. Not that the thought isn't tempting, but I've decided the best thing I can do to thank you is to help you lighten up a little, have some fun."

No way. "That's not necessary."

"You mightn't think so, but don't knock it until you've tried it." She stroked her hand over his cheek and ran a finger over his lips.

He shivered, unable to hold back his body's reaction.

"When I'm finished with you, you'll be so relaxed you won't know yourself."

That's what he was worried about.

Finally he managed to break the spell and stand. "Corey, I insist. It's not necessary, and I'd rather not."

She didn't bat an eyelid. *Oh she is good – she should be a barrister.*

"Don't be too hasty, James. We'll talk tomorrow and get started."

A swish of cool air touched his face as she stood up and breezed out of the door. Turning around to face him, her eyes alight with laughter, she winked again. "Don't look so worried. It'll the best fun you've ever had."

He stared at the door for several minutes after she had left. What the heck had he gotten himself into?

Chapter Two

Damn the gods. The shadowy figure followed Corey all the way home. She'd managed to extricate herself from the police much too quickly. *It must be that damn lawyer.* He glided just above the rooflines, deliberately ducking behind buildings so he could mask his presence. It appeared that here, in modern times, lawyers were as inconvenient and annoying as they were on Mt Olympus. Terpsichore thought she was free and clear, but only he knew it to be a false sense of security. *Let her feel comfortable for a while longer. Soon she will wish herself back in that police cell,* because his plans for her meant only fear and pain. His plan was foolproof. Using the mortals he'd created so long ago was a stroke of genius, and would anger Zeus further, allowing him to exact his revenge in the most painful way possible.

* * * *

Corey smiled as she stripped off her bra and panties and stepped into the warming spray of her shower. As she remembered her visit with James, her skin tingled and hundreds of tiny goose bumps appeared. She wanted more.

He'd tried really hard to appear conservative on the surface, but she knew better. From the minute she'd seen him enter that interrogation room, she'd known he had more than met the eye. And he was oh so easy on the eye. To be more accurate, he was beautiful. The combination of blond hair and broad shoulders appealed, but the kindness she saw in his eyes and the loyalty he displayed to his friends touched something inside her. That surprised her, considering her rather checkered history with men. In her home on Mount Olympus, she couldn't ever remember feeling anything more than amusement for men. In fact, she cringed when she remembered how she'd used them for her own fun more often than not, never caring about their feelings. She felt an overwhelming sense of shame. *What a selfish, self-centered bitch.*

As she toweled herself dry, Corey pondered how Hera had done her the biggest favor of her life by sending her here. Hera had thought of the banishment as punishment, but, ironically, it had become more of a learning experience. Much to her surprise she was turning into a different person. A better person, she hoped, because when she looked back at her former life she didn't like what she saw.

As she slipped into bed, she felt the cool smoothness of the silk sheets over her bare skin. Her thoughts moved once again to the man on her mind. Maybe her new-found need to be a better person was what drew her to him. She sensed his innate goodness, even with his obvious discomfort at helping her. He wasn't like any man she had met before. He didn't help her for her own sake, he did it for Susan. That showed a huge amount of respect and loyalty for his friend. Of course, that wasn't the only thing that attracted her. That amazing body made her sigh, and the fact that he kissed better than all her former lovers put together certainly helped.

So what if he wasn't all that excited about her thanking him some more. Her efforts to be a better person didn't include taking no for an answer. She was doing it for him—he just didn't know it yet. *Oh yes*, she thought as she slipped into a relaxed sleep filled with sexy dreams. This promised to be so much fun.

Look out, James, because Corey is on a mission.

* * * *

A cool westerly wind blew several strands of Corey's untamable hair across her face. She tucked the unruly curls behind her ear while slipping her key in the door with her free hand. Her first dance class didn't start for a few hours yet, but she planned on getting ready for a special surprise she had in store later on for James. She didn't even stop to worry about how she could get him to her dance studio. Now that her powers were finally returning she might as well use them for good instead of nastiness. Being a goddess had some advantages, after all, and although it probably wasn't sporting to use her talents to plant the thought of contacting her in his mind, she promised herself not to use her magic after this. Once he got a taste of how much fun life could be, he'd thank her.

Of course he would. He'd been brought up well. He'd thank her in a mutually satisfying manner. She traced a finger across her bottom lip and relived the moment of his kiss. Explosive came to mind, but such a mild word to describe the moment of contact. They say you have to watch the quiet ones.

They were right.

She daydreamed all the way through the vacuuming and mopping of the dance floor, and couldn't remember dusting the window ledges and furniture, but an hour later, when she'd lit candles all around the room, the transformation was amazing. Maybe she should kiss a lawyer more often? It seemed like a great way to get the cleaning done. Goodness knows it had taken her long enough to learn how to fend for herself. She used to just wave her hand and it would all be done, but here, in this time, there were no servants, and she hadn't been able to use her powers—until now. She might be finding her former talents, but she actually liked looking after herself. Dare she say she even liked housework? Weird though the thought was, now that she was regaining her former powers, she wasn't sure she wanted to use them that much. Besides, she could never tell when some mortal would walk in and catch her in the act. How the heck would she explain that away? These mortals didn't seem very open-minded when it came to magic, and they certainly weren't ready to see her using it. Not yet anyway.

* * * *

After the last class had finally finished, Corey blessed the foresight of having a shower installed at the dance studio. After sliding the mop broom around to touch up the floor, she entered the bathroom, undressed and turned on the water. She sighed as the cool spray ran over her sweat-slicked body. The water started doing its magic.

Thunk.

What was that? She turned the tap off and inclined her head toward the door, but heard nothing more.

Maybe it was the wind, and the anticipation of dancing with James making her jumpy. It shouldn't because she had no doubt he would be there. The package she'd sent to his office contained an enchanted note planted deep in a box where no one else could touch it. He would come to her, she knew it. Her body tingled at the thought and she smiled at herself in the mirror as she dressed. Her body was looking pretty damn good, and her clothes accentuated her curves in all the right places. It had been a long time since she'd had this much fun. She shivered. Oh yes…the anticipation. She couldn't wait.

She'd chosen a demure, but deceptively seductive dress. It covered her skin completely, but through the swirls of aquamarine and black flowers, it clung to her curves like a second skin—so much so that James was in for a surprise when he ran his hand over her back. She giggled, thinking of his conservative self—shocked by her lack of underwear. *Oh yes, he is going to get an education he will never forget.*

At the loud knock on the front door she stopped breathing. *He's here.*

She left the bathroom and all but ran to get to the door. But a few steps into the studio she stopped dead…and screamed bloody murder.

* * * *

After parking his car on the street in front of the dance studio, James shook his head. What was he doing here? Before the package had arrived he'd already decided not to see Corey again. It hadn't been an easy decision to make considering the restless night he'd spent dreaming about her amazing body, those unusual eyes, and the promises her kiss had hinted at. She'd told him she would thank him in more fun ways, but he had intended to politely refuse. Burying himself in work all day unfortunately had failed to quell the memories of her scorching mouth and the feel of her body pressed against his. *I've got it bad.* Maybe that explained why the minute he'd smelled her perfume in the box and touched the smooth paper of the invitation, all he could think about was seeing her again. He'd convinced himself he could get her out of his system if he saw her one more time. God, he hoped he was right.

He admitted to being curious to see what she had planned. The vague note said something about taking two to tango, or something equally cliché. The little he knew of Corey guaranteed that, whatever she was up to, she wouldn't be an average date. He smiled at that thought.

Checking out the street, he was surprised to see such a quiet neighborhood. He'd had visions of nightclubs and sex shops, and this tidy strip of shopfronts certainly didn't fit that picture.

He stood back and inspected the tasteful signage announcing 'Terpsichore's Tango'. Terpsichore? The Greek Muse of Dance? He remembered his ancient history classes, and the mythological group of beautiful women who'd inspired the people of Olympus. She definitely had the looks, and she'd inspired some rather creative dreams last night. Yes, the name certainly fitted.

A loud scream came from inside her studio. *What the – ?*

His hand shook as he tried the handle, but it wouldn't budge. He shouted through the door. "Corey? Are you okay? Let me in."

No answer. He slapped his hand on the wood, with no effect. Next he tried butting his shoulder against the door – he put all his weight behind it and shoved. It took three attempts before the old wood surrounding the lock started to give. He stood back and kicked the door in, slamming it against the wall behind, causing the glass in the window to shatter. He raised his hand to prevent the door flinging back into him while he moved quickly inside to check on Corey.

He found her standing frozen in place, staring at a grotesque body hanging from the ceiling.

Fuck!

As he drew closer he was relieved to see that it wasn't a real body, but an effigy of Corey, and the doll appeared to be strangled. He called her name, but Corey didn't react. He raced to her side, and pulled her into his arms, turning her away from the ugly sight in front of her.

He looked around the studio, and spying a door to the left, he led Corey into a small sitting room.

"Sit down and catch your breath while I call the police." He flipped open his phone to dial the number, but Corey placed her hand on his forearm.

Her eyes implored him. "No. Please, no police."

He helped her to sit down on the small couch. "We should report this. I'm a solicitor, I'm obliged to call it in."

She touched his arm again as he sat next to her. "I've already spent enough time with the police over the last few days. I don't need to draw any more of their attention."

He grasped her icy hands between his and rubbed gently. "I can understand that, but listen to me, Corey, this was more than just a sick joke. We need help to find out who did this."

Her eyes pleaded with him to leave it alone. "It was probably kids."

He shook his head. "I don't think so. What if it's the jerk who caused you all that trouble yesterday? He needs to be stopped. We can't let him get away with that."

"But what if it's not him?"

She shivered, despite his efforts to warm her. He scanned the room, spying a coat hanging on a hook near the front door. He placed her hands gently back into her lap, then stood and grabbed the coat. He slipped it over her shoulders and pulled the sides together. Her breath brushed against him, sending shivers over his skin and he fought the urge to pull her into his arms again. "Even if it is a kids' prank, we need to let their parents know."

"I'm sorry, James. I can't face the police again. Not tonight." Her eyes filled with unshed tears. He saw fear, but underneath he also glimpsed a stubborn streak a mile long. Sighing, he realized she wouldn't give in, no matter how many logical and legal arguments he used. "Fine. I'll go and cut the doll down and check out a few things. Will you be okay in here while I'm gone?"

She flashed him a brave smile, visibly relaxing as she leaned back in the chair. What she didn't know was that he planned to show the doll to a detective he knew. He couldn't let this go without first making some effort to find the culprit. They may try again and she could be in grave danger.

The doll was strung up over the exposed beam that ran across the ceiling of the studio. The rope was a thick plastic twine, not unlike the type used to tie a load of rubbish on the back of a trailer. Easing the ghoulish figure down to the floor, James was careful not to touch the mannequin more than needed. He frowned as he looked at the horrible purple face where a fake crimson tongue had been sewn in, flapping about like it was alive. The wig consisted of long red curls in a macabre facsimile of Corey's wild hair. It was impossible not to see this as a threat. It didn't matter what Corey said, he couldn't let this go. He would find out was who was doing this, and why. He was a Barrington, and Barringtons didn't leave women in danger. To be truthful, he couldn't speak for his cousins, but he knew that *he* didn't.

It took only a few minutes to carry the light bundle to the trunk of his car. He returned to find Corey still huddled on the seat. She looked up as he entered the room. He was struck by how fragile she looked sitting there all alone, clinging to the edges of her coat as it hung loosely over her shoulders. He barely knew her, but in the short time since they'd met, he'd seen her as someone always in control, and definitely a woman who knew what she wanted and went for it. Now she appeared vulnerable and unsure of herself. The urge was strong to wrap her up in his arms and reassure her that everything would be okay, but he held back. A relationship with her was not on the table, and he didn't want to give her the wrong impression. In her fragile state, she deserved honesty. As he drew closer she looked up, her eyes shimmering, but determined.

"You're my hero—again. I don't know how I'm going to ever repay you, James."

He sucked in his top lip and stared at the ceiling. "No payment necessary. I'm only doing what anyone would do."

She stood, offering the coat for him to hold open for her. As she slid her arms in, she looked over her shoulder. "Not everyone is as caring as you are. It's a rare thing, don't diminish it."

After looping the last button, she reached up and softly kissed his cheek. "Don't stress or go reading anything more into this. I'm an affectionate person and I like to reward good deeds."

Resisting the urge to grab her by those shoulders and show her a real kiss, he pulled his car keys out of his pocket and stepped away. She reminded him of what he wasn't ready to accept. He didn't need her kind of reward in his life right now. His promise to his father didn't allow for it. So why did his mouth go dry thinking about what form her reward might take? He cleared his throat as she buttoned up her coat. "Do you want to have a bite to eat? Take your mind off things for a while?" His voice cracked as he spoke. *Oh great.* What the devil was happening to him? Where was his legendary control? God, he hoped she didn't notice. She didn't need any more encouragement and neither did a certain part of his anatomy.

Her hand touched his shoulder. "James?"

"Yes?" He cleared his throat, feeling the heat from her touch burning through his jacket. "So, are we on for dinner?"

She smiled, showing him she knew exactly what he'd been thinking. His heart rate kicked up a couple of notches.

"That would be lovely, James. Lead on."

* * * *

Garlic and red wine.

The closest thing to ambrosia this world provided. Corey breathed in the heady aroma of the luscious sauces and sighed. Oh yes, she would have to take some of her favorite things from this world back with her—if she ever got back home. James might be uptight a lot of the time, but he knew his food and wine. The small trattoria bustled with a crowd of diners, but the maître d' smiled widely, finding them a small table near the rear terrace. A portly waiter flapped a crisp white tablecloth over the table with a flick of his wrists and produced a single red rose in a vase for decoration. He refused to let Corey seat herself, insisting on holding her chair out and seating her himself.

"We are honored to have such a *bella* lady in our midst this fine evening."

He kissed the air above her fingers as she pulled her hand away. Catching a glimpse of James' face out of the corner of her eye, she almost laughed out loud at the scowl he aimed at the flamboyant Italian. "You are good for my ego, *signore*. I might come here again, if only to hear more of your compliments."

James grunted, placing his hands on the table. "I'd like a bottle of your best Merlot, two glasses and a couple of menus, please."

The waiter continued staring at Corey while he answered. "Right away, sir."

Corey giggled as the waiter stayed rooted to his spot. Spying his name tag, she leaned forward. "Umm... Bruno?"

He snapped out of his daze and blushed. "Oh, yes. I'm sorry, I will get the wine." He bowed with a flourish to Corey and winked. "I shall return in a few minutes."

James watched him with serious eyes as he walked over to the bar and selected a bottle of wine and two glasses. "I suppose you get that a lot."

Many times. She smiled wistfully. It had been some time since she'd experienced it. Men watched her dance, but this was different. This type of adoration was harmless. It felt good, and she needed the boost. "Not lately, but it's flattering, and I must admit it's good for my ego," she smiled. "I never knock back a good compliment. Does it bother you?"

He shook his head a little bit too quickly. "No. Why should it?"

Tucking a few loose tendrils of hair behind her ear, she sat back in her seat. *Oh yes, it does.* Even so, he denied it, but she could see it made him uncomfortable. Maybe he wasn't so immune to her after all? She smiled back at him. "That's good, because I'd hate it to ruin our dinner."

He reached across the table and touched her cheek. "I'm being a jerk, aren't I? I should be cheering you up, not acting like a dickhead."

She leaned into his warm palm, soothed by the feel of his surprisingly soft skin. "You're doing fine. I feel better already."

James removed his hand as Bruno returned with the wine and the menus. He tasted the small amount poured into his glass, and nodded, prompting him to fill both their glasses. How Bruno didn't spill any was a mystery to her as the smiling Italian didn't look away from Corey's face the whole time. James raised his glass and offered a silent toast toward Corey and

Bruno finally got the message and stood back from the table, breaking his stare and turning to James.

"The specials tonight are grilled scampi with melted garlic butter, and fettuccine alla Calabrese."

James arched his brow. "Corey?"

Oh yummy. "Oh, they both sound so delicious. I'll have the scampi please."

"It's for two, madame. Would the gentleman like to share?"

"That's fine. We'll share."

"Are you sure, James? I can have something else if you don't like scampi. I don't mind."

He smiled at her across the table. "It's your night. Besides, I love to share, as long as it's large enough that we both get to enjoy it."

Bruno nodded, bowing to them both as he backed away. "As you wish."

* * * *

Corey moaned with pleasure from the first bite. *The scampi is so delicious it should be illegal.* She closed her eyes and savored the light texture dripping with lightly flavored butter. Licking each of her fingers to catch the drips, she opened her eyes again and looked directly into James' face. Her skin heated as her eyes met his. *Maybe there is hope for him yet.* Scooping up a forkful of the delicate scampi flesh, she offered it to him, who surprised her by grabbing her wrist as he slowly drew the luscious piece of seafood into his mouth. Using his thumb, he traced circles across her skin as his lips encircled the fork.

My goddess, is it getting hot in here or what? Two could play at that game. She plucked a small pile of the delicate flesh with her fingers and gestured for him to take it from her hand. "Now you feed me."

His eyes widened but he didn't miss a beat as he took the offering and placed it near her lips. She opened her mouth a little and sucked in the tasty gift. She was surprised when he followed it with his finger. She lapped on the salty skin, licking the tip. He groaned as he withdrew his hand, knocking his glass over, spilling red wine all over the tablecloth and splashing his shirt.

"Shit!" He jumped to his feet, grabbing the napkin and furiously mopping at the growing red stain. Bruno raced over with a jug of water and flicked some water at it with his hand.

"Careful, mate. Get me some soda water and a towel, don't drown me."

Corey couldn't help herself, she laughed out loud.

James, on the other hand, didn't seem to share the humor as he glared at her. "What are you laughing at?"

For his benefit she stopped laughing, but was unable to keep the smile at bay. "You have to admit, it was pretty funny."

"Glad I could give you some entertainment," he said, his face betraying just a hint of a smile, giving her hope that he wasn't too uptight to see the humor in the situation.

"I'm sorry, James, you know I'm only teasing. If you take me back to my place, I can rinse that stain out."

He flashed her a relieved smile. "Sounds like a plan. I'll pay the check."

The trip to her cottage seemed to take forever since James wasn't in much of a mood for talking. She really had a job ahead of her to cheer him up, but she wasn't worried. She'd never failed before and she wasn't about to start now.

She closed her eyes and thought about what she had planned. Hopefully he got with the program, because her lips tingled just thinking about another mind-blowing kiss. Before this night finished, she was determined they would do more than kiss. If she was wrong, she might have to face the unpalatable fact that she was losing her touch. What had started out as an exercise in gratitude had quickly turned into something more. She sensed his hidden depths and that underneath that conservative exterior he burnt with a heat she wanted to share. She wanted *him*. Not just the sex.

Judging by the way he jerked the car to a stop outside her house, she had her work cut out for her. She didn't know why he was fighting their attraction, but she'd keep trying to get through to him. Hopefully in a short while he'd be distracted.

The Victorian cottage she called home was her pride and joy, but right now she tried to remember the state the house had been in when she'd left that morning, hoping it was one of her good days. *Too late to worry about it now.* The door opened and the scent of her favorite oils wafted out. *At least it smells okay.*

She pushed the door open and walked inside. She led James to the back of the house, which had a large open living area, and included the kitchen and a guest bathroom. Bookshelves spread over one wall while two large chintz couches faced each other in the center of the room. Turning around, she smiled, watching James follow her in.

She gestured to his shirt. "If you take that off, I'll soak it for you. I hear cold soda water does wonders."

His eyes narrowed as he removed his jacket, throwing it over a chair before he quickly undid the buttons. As he started to shuck it off, Corey moved and stopped him. "Wait, let me do that."

His nostrils flared and he sucked in a breath. Dropping his arms to his side, he smiled.

"Sure. Go for it."

The heat sizzled beneath her fingers as she slid the shirt off his shoulders. Tiny currents arced into her hands and spread the warmth along her arms and into her torso. *This guy makes me seriously hot.* Her voice was raspy when she spoke. "I thought you were in a bad mood."

The intensity of his stare increased as he held her eyes captive. "I got over it."

Yes! "I'm glad."

As the shirt drifted to the floor, she bent to retrieve it but James stopped her, pulling her upright again.

"Don't start something you don't intend to finish, Corey."

"Oh, I definitely intend to finish, James." A muscle flickered in his face as she traced her finger across his jaw. "Hang on to that thought while I put your shirt in the sink. Pour yourself a drink and I'll be back in a jiffy."

My goddess, it hasn't taken him long to get in the mood. How did that happen? She hadn't used any of her powers and he'd still been a bit miffed when they'd pulled up. It looked like someone had interfered, but who could that be? She lived in a different world now — no one from her former life had found their way to her before. Not so far anyway. *This reminds me of the tricks Eros used to play, but he's happily married to Psyche now and apparently over his childish games, so it couldn't be him, could it?*

43

"Why not, sweet cheeks?"

She dropped the shirt in the sink and grabbed the sides for support. She knew that voice.

"Eros?"

"Turn around and look, babe."

Spinning around, she screamed with delight and hurled herself at the tall, blond giant who was her best friend.

"Hey, give me some room here, babe. I need to breathe."

"I'm sorry, Erie, I'm just so happy to see you. How did you get here?"

"Shouldn't that be *why* am I here?"

"Okay, why are you here?"

"Zeus tracked you down. And since I come here occasionally, he asked me to keep an eye on you."

Her heart stopped. She wasn't ready to leave her new life. Not yet anyway. "So, are you here to take me back home?"

"I can't do that, my sweet Terpsichore. The pathway to return lies within your own heart."

That sounded better. She could control it herself. "How?" she asked.

"That is for you to discover."

"Cut the crap, you double-talking doofus. Tell me what I need to do."

"I can't tell you. I mean it when I say you have to come home yourself. I don't know how it happens, I'm just the messenger."

"Oh great. Another of Zeus' riddles to solve."

"Hera, not your father, cast the spell. Your father sent me here to check on you. You must take care, Terpsichore. There are Titan rebels loose in this world."

"I haven't seen any so far, but at the moment I'm more interested in what you did to James out there."

He laughed. "You are beginning to sound like the others in this place. I gave him a little nudge, my sweet. He's not going to do anything he didn't already want to do in his heart."

"Damn it, Erie, I haven't used my powers that way since I've been here. I'd rather he acted of his own accord."

With a nonchalant shrug he waved his hand. "Fine, I've returned him to his previous state. Good luck, my friend."

"I'm sure I can handle it. I can handle my father, can't I?"

"Good point."

She hadn't realized how good it would feel to speak to someone from home, but seeing him reminded her how much she missed her family—especially her father. "How long are you here in this world? Can we talk later?"

He winked. "Sure thing, precious. I'll be back soon, but be sure to leave a 'do not disturb' sign on the bedroom door if you have company."

She smiled. "If I still have my touch, you can guarantee it."

His face sobered. "Be careful, Terpsichore. There are evil forces afoot."

"Don't be so dramatic, Eros."

His voice softened. "I mean it, Corey. Don't say I didn't warn you."

With a flourish, he snapped his fingers and disappeared.

Corey sighed and took a clean breath to prepare for the return of James' bad mood. He faced the double doors that led out to the back garden, his back to her.

He turned as she approached and moved toward her, so close she could smell his spicy scent.

"What took you so long?" His presence seemed to fill the whole room, overwhelming her.

"I—"

He wrapped his arms around her then pulled her against his hard chest—his naked, hard chest.

Tilting her chin upwards with his index finger, he studied her face. "You need to be faster next time."

Before she could get a word in, he swooped down and captured her lips.

Eros must have done this, the bastard.

However, her anger dissipated when pure unadulterated lust took over. He plundered her mouth with his clever tongue gaining entry and taking everything he wanted. He touched her, moving his hands in all directions and sending tingles of sensation over every path they took. His body radiated power and the primal scent of his bare skin aroused her more than she had ever thought possible.

James skimmed a hand over her hip and lower to the edge of her skirt. Her breath hitched. When he skimmed over the bare flesh of her thigh with his hand, her favorite spot did a happy dance. The skirt lifted higher and higher and she forgot to breathe entirely.

He was taking control and she didn't mind in the least. This was not like her at all.

Moving his attention from her mouth, he trailed a path of kisses along her jaw to her ear. His warm breath sent shivers along her body as he whispered, "Do you always leave home without any underwear, or is it just for my benefit?"

She came apart in his arms as he inched closer to his target. Those little sighs almost finished him before he'd even begun. *Why did this woman make him lose control?* Never in all his experiences with women had he been so turned on so fast.

As he dipped his fingers intimately, her muscles contracted, pulling him further in. *God, he wanted to know what that felt like, to be inside her.*

Slow down. Jeez, he didn't know how she'd gotten under his skin so quickly, or how close he came to exploding, but he didn't want to leave it half done. Deep down he knew this would be his only chance with Corey. She didn't belong in his world, or he in hers, but at least they had tonight and he wanted it to be good for both of them.

She tugged at his fly.

"Easy now, girl, I want to last long enough for you to enjoy it. If you keep that up, it'll be all over in a few seconds."

She sucked in a breath as he moved back, removing his hands so he could lift her dress over her head.

He stared at her, his breathing ragged. The perfection of her body took his breath away. "Oh God, you're so beautiful."

She drew his pants and boxers down to his ankles. "Fair's fair. Now we're even."

She took a step back and stared, looking him up and down from his face to his chest and his groin, then back again. He didn't realize it was possible, but he grew even harder.

"You're not so bad yourself, James."

After he had removed his shoes and socks she took his hand and led him to her bedroom, stopping to turn on the muted lighting by her dresser. When they reached the edge of her bed, she raised her hands and pulled his face closer, kissing him on the mouth. He wrapped his arms around her and deepened the kiss, tasting the wine they'd shared at dinner as he explored her mouth and drew her in further.

They moved to the bed, lying side by side, touching, feeling, kissing. She rolled onto her back and he followed her, his body on top. Their eyes met and he smiled.

"Touch me, James," she said.

"Anything you want, beautiful." He kissed her again before he began a slow trail down to her breasts. Nuzzling the valley in between, he inhaled her amazing perfume.

Exotic and erotic.

As he licked around one areola, her nipple tightened. He nipped gently at the end with his teeth. She groaned, urging him on, and he turned his attention to the other breast.

"Oooh…yes."

With each touch, the fire built inside him. Moving down her body, he zeroed in on her clit and stroked it with his tongue. He slid his finger inside her, smiling at her happy sigh. She squeezed his shoulders, urging him on. He slid in another finger and circled some more.

"Does that feel good?"

She groaned. Loudly. *Oh God.*

He moved above her, teasing her, rubbing back and forth across her skin.

"Oh yes — there!"

He chuckled, then slid down her body and tasted her, smiling when she gripped his head to hold him in place.

"Don't stop!" she cried out.

He kept up the assault, and from the sound of her sighs, he was taking her exactly where he wanted her to go. She started to shudder and shake, and he figured it was time for more action.

"I can't wait anymore," he growled.

"Thank the goddess! Neither can I," she laughed.

He reached over to grab his wallet and retrieved a condom. In a microsecond he'd ripped open the packet and sheathed himself before he plunged deep inside.

Her muscles clenched tightly around him.

"Oh God, Corey."

He moved slowly out, then entered her again, building a slow rhythm. He strained to rein in the pace as his intention was to make it good for her, but he wasn't sure how long he could keep that up.

"Move with me, Corey."

She did, and it was amazing, the heat and moisture an unbeatable combination.

He took hold of her hands and moved her arms behind her head, holding them steady. He rocked into her, whispering in her ear, telling her what he wanted to do to her as he shifted slightly so he could go deeper. *Holy shit she was so tight!*

Corey twisted below him, sliding and shifting and grunting at the same time as she joined him past the point of no return.

She arched her back, crying out as she came, their sweat-soaked bodies moved together, until they both collapsed, side by side, exhausted but sated. As their breathing calmed, he drew her close, trapping her with his leg, and gently stroked her silky skin. He kissed her cheek and relaxed for the first time in a long time.

* * * *

He stayed awake for hours, enjoying being with Corey. She stirred as he ran a finger over her arm and the sweet sighing noises she made had him wanting her all over again.

He sighed, remembering why this wasn't a good idea. With his workload, added to his promise to his father, there wasn't a lot of room for her in his life. He couldn't see her playing second fiddle either, but he still couldn't get her out of his head, and it confused the heck out of him. She was gorgeous—anyone would be attracted to her—but it went beyond attraction, and he couldn't explain it exactly. If he allowed himself to become more involved, leaving her would be horrible for them both. He didn't want to hurt her that way, so he'd do something before it got to that point. He hoped she would forgive him for what he was about to do, because he wasn't sure he would forgive himself.

Of course it went without saying that he would continue to make sure she was safe. He wouldn't be able to live with himself otherwise. He would call in a few favors with some cops he knew, getting her some protection at least. There was also the matter of that mannequin in his trunk. Once he handed that over to the cops he could back out with a clear conscience. *So why did that thought leave a bad taste in his mouth?*

He looked down at her gorgeous face, and planted a gentle kiss on her swollen lips. Her lips came alive and she slid her arms around his neck.

"Hey..."

"Hey, yourself."

Even her bed hair was gorgeous, he thought as she smiled up at him.

"Wanna fool around some more?"

Surely one more time won't hurt? "What did you have in mind?"

In one quick move, she flipped him on his back and straddled him. "I figure it's my turn to be the boss." She leaned forward and licked a trail across his chest. "Do you have a problem with that, James?"

Blood raced from his chest to his lower anatomy in record time. "Not that I can think of," he replied, his voice strangled.

"Good." She laughed at him, a sexy gleam in her eye. "I have plans for you."

"Plans?"

She grinned wickedly before leaning forward and sliding up and back over his skin, working her way down his thighs. He came to life in her hands as she stroked. The pleasure was so intense he almost blacked out. Her mouth covered him with a soft warmth that both enticed and aroused. She tongued, sucked and teased until he didn't think he could take any more, then she ripped open a foil packet and covered him with the condom, before she lifted herself over him and slid slowly down his shaft. He howled. Loudly.

"I think you've done this before," he said when his voice came back.

She frowned, suddenly serious. "But never before with you, James. It's never been like this."

He touched her cheek. "Hey, I didn't mean that the way it sounded."

"I know what you meant." She smiled wickedly at him. "Now lie back and enjoy."

He grinned back at her as he lay down on the pillow. "Yes, ma'am."

She leaned forward, rubbing her breasts against his chest before leaning back just a little, and offering him a breast. He kissed the rosy peak before sucking the nipple inside his mouth. She moved, and he moaned as she shifted back and forth on his lap, riding him well and good. The tension in his body was rising but just before he reached the point of no return she slowed down.

"Hey, I'm dying here."

She gave him a wicked smile. "The wait will do you good. Be patient, it'll be worth it."

She sat upright, her body a picture of beauty. "Look at me, James."

When she rubbed her hands over her body and breasts he felt his body twitch inside her. "I'm looking, but I won't last much longer if you keep that up."

She laughed as she leaned forward again and kissed him and all thought left as she began the triple assault on his senses. Her mouth was magic itself as she explored him with her tongue and sucked on his bottom lip. The electric touch of her skin rubbing against his was unlike any sensation he had experienced before, and with her in the driving seat, squeezing and moving back and forth over him, he really thought he'd died and gone to heaven.

He lifted his hips to meet her and she moaned.

"Oh goddess, yes!"

Their bodies were in a haze of movement and heavy breathing as she came around him, squeezing him so tight he couldn't wait any longer and followed her with the most amazing orgasm ever.

He'd better be careful or he could get used to this.

Chapter Three

Corey woke to sunlight blazing through her bedroom window. She sighed, stretching her arms over her head and turned to smile at James. Only he wasn't there.

Strange. This did not feel good.

She slipped off the bed, and reached for her robe, tying the belt tightly around her waist as she walked out into the kitchen. The knot in her stomach grew.

"James?"

No answer.

She closed her eyes and listened. He was gone. No goodbye, no note. Gone.

Great.

Working on automatic pilot, she filled the kettle with water for a cup of tea before sitting on the stool at the breakfast bench.

How could I have got it so wrong? The best sex she'd had in several lifetimes and she'd fooled herself into believing it was more than that. She'd been convinced he felt the same way she did.

He'd been so passionate, but so gentle. Plus the way he'd supported her through the whole hanging mannequin incident must mean he cared something for her. Or so she'd thought. It had been more than sex, she was sure of it.

So why would he run out on her like that? Whatever the reason, she wasn't a goddess of the arts for nothing. She was creative. All she needed was a plan to show him he needed her in his life.

What am I doing? She couldn't use her powers, it wouldn't be right. If he didn't want her for herself, she didn't want him at all. And that's what scared her more than anything. She'd never got emotionally involved before. *What was different now?*

She'd changed in the months since she'd been banished by Hera. Having to fend for herself had forced her to realize what a self-centered and totally self-indulgent spoiled brat she'd always been. Watching how these mortals willingly worked to better themselves added a new perspective. The kindness of the people who had helped her since she'd arrived in this alien and confusing world humbled her, whereas her past behavior left her ashamed. But her memories of Olympus were not all bad. Traveling with her family and Apollo to entertain the courts and inspire the artists was fun. She missed her sisters, particularly Calliope, who loved to play tricks on their other siblings.

If she made it home, things would be different. She wouldn't still be taking advantage of her position to get her own way, that was for sure. She would reward those who served her and honor those who pledged their loyalty. She'd also encourage her whole family to do the same.

She thought back to Eros' visit the night before. *What was he up to?* That warning about Titan rebels had to be a ruse, surely. *What would a Titan rebel want with her?* She wasn't in her homeland, so her position and powers meant nothing here. It must be an excuse to play some mischief. Eros was her friend, but he loved to play jokes. Over time, she'd learned to take what he said with a grain of salt. His little game the night before was proof that he continued to love playing tricks.

She sighed, as she thought about last night. If only she could be sure the feelings she'd sensed in James had come from his own free will, and had not been enhanced by Eros' spells.

There was no use dwelling on it. She needed a new plan of attack. Moreover, she should figure out what she was going to do with James once she'd won him. *Was this love?* She didn't know, but her heart was telling her she'd never cared about someone as much as she cared about James. As a firm believer in fate, she knew deep down that James was her destiny. He just didn't know it yet.

* * * *

The taxi driver was one of those who talked so much he didn't take a breath while he told her his life story. Corey's normal exuberant self usually liked chatting back, but today all she felt was irritation. It wasn't the cab driver's fault. When she'd walked out of her house, she'd remembered that James had driven her home and her car was still at her work.

She was relieved when the driver had finished his tirade on how the government wasn't doing enough for the working classes, and stopped the cab in front of the dance studio. She paid her fare and stood on the footpath, inhaling the delicious aroma of freshly ground coffee. She checked her watch and realized that her first class didn't start for another forty-five minutes, so she crossed the street and made her way to the local coffee shop.

Coffee in hand, she headed back toward the studio. A car sped toward her, veering from side to side along the road. She stood there, stunned, like a deer caught in headlights. She couldn't breathe, her heart pounded and her limbs wouldn't work. The world moved in slow motion until someone called out and she realized she was about to be hit if she didn't do something, and fast. She threw her body to the ground between two parked cars and, landed on her knees, hot coffee spilling all over her as the offending car sped off in the distance.

"Are you okay, Corey?" She looked up as George, the owner of the coffee shop, took her arm and helped her to her feet.

"I think so." Her voice shook. "Let me catch my breath."

"Come and sit in my café. I'll get you another coffee, on the house."

She looked down at her stained clothes and bloody knees and sighed.

"Thank you for the offer, George, but I've just lost my appetite for coffee. I think I'll get to the studio and clean myself up a bit instead.

He looked down at her ripped stockings and gasped.

"Holy cow, Corey. You're wounded!"

She glanced at the small grazes and laughed. "I think I can handle a few grazes."

"Okay, if you're sure, but I'll still walk you to your door. We don't want any more mishaps, now, do we?"

"You're very sweet, George," she said as she shook her hands to free the grass clippings sticking to the wet coffee on her skin. "Tell me, George, how come all the good men are married?"

He flushed red to the roots of his gray hair and laughed. "Don't you let my Maria hear you. My wife, she is a very jealous woman."

She laughed as they reached her door. "I'll keep that in mind."

She turned to him, her voice still a little shaky. "Thanks for your help, George. I'll be fine now."

"You take care. It looked to me like that car deliberately tried to run you down. You should call the police."

No way. Not after the last few days. "No, no police. I'm sure it was just some hooligans out for a joyride. Anyway, they're long gone. What can the police do now?"

He sighed. "I suppose. I wish I'd gotten the whole number plate, though, but I did get part of it if you change your mind. I'd better get back to the café. Are you sure you're okay?"

"I'll be fine." She plastered her best reassuring smile onto her face. "Thanks for your help. I can take it from here."

Somehow, she managed to get the key in the lock and get inside without falling over. Once there, she slumped against the closed door and slid to the floor. *Oh shit!* Someone had tried to kill her. She knew that now, despite what she'd told George. Two threats in two days was definitely no coincidence. If she counted that weird trumped-up charge from the night before, she was three for three in the bad luck stakes. Maybe Eros wasn't joking after all. She stared at her hands as she held them out in front of her.

Oh goddess, I'm shaking like a leaf.

"I told you to be careful."

She jumped. "Eros?"

Her best friend stood in front of her, grinning like an idiot. "The one and only."

"Bloody hell, Erie, you scared the pants off me."

He looked her up and down. "No, I didn't, but if you want some help to finish the job, I can oblige."

She shrugged. Joking wasn't high on her list of priorities at the moment. "Whatever."

"Sorry, Corey, some habits are hard to break. You know I don't mean it."

"I hope Psyche doesn't know you're still using your old lines."

"She knows, but she trusts me. It's all part of my charm. Besides, I would never betray her. She's the love of my life."

Corey thought of James, and for the first time in her life could relate to the idea of fidelity. "I know, and I'm happy for you," she said as she hugged him. "But can you help me out and tell me what's going on?"

Eros waved his hand in the air and in no time at all Corey found herself seated on her couch.

Head spinning, she grabbed hold of the armrest to steady herself as she landed. "Jeez, I forgot you could do that. Warn me next time, won't you?"

Eros raised his eyebrows and snickered. "You really are becoming one of them, aren't you? Forgetting to use your powers, speaking like a common mortal. Soon you'll forget completely that you're a goddess. You are Terpsichore, the Muse of Dance"

"Eros, how can I ever forget? I'm stuck here in this place so I have to blend in." She pulled her skirt up and grimaced when she saw the blood dripping off her grazed knees. "You think I sound like one of them? Cool."

"See, that's what I mean. Since when did a Muse use words such as 'cool'?"

She poked her tongue out at him.

"When you do that, you look like them, too. Disgusting! Now let's get to the reason why I'm here."

She lay back against the couch. "Please do. And while you're at it, you can apologize for zapping James last night when I particularly asked you not to."

Eros slapped a hand against his chest. "I'm deeply affronted, Terpsichore. I did nothing of the sort. After I removed that little nudge, I left him alone, just as you asked." His eyes lit with mirth. "Oh, I see... He and you?"

"None of your business."

But he wouldn't let it go. "You and James? Horizontal folk dancing?"

"Now who's talking like a mortal?"

"All right, I get the message. Now to why I am here."

"Pass me a wet cloth from the bathroom first, will you?"

He shook his head. "Tsk, tsk... You've really forgotten, haven't you?"

He snapped his fingers and her knees tingled. And just like that her wounds vanished.

She hadn't remembered she could have done that herself.

"Thanks, Eros, though I'm not sure you should be throwing the magic around so freely. In this world, you don't know what entity might be attracted to the cosmos."

"Actually, it's evil entities that bring me here to see you."

"Last night you mentioned something about Titan rebels?"

He nodded. "Titan rebels have threatened Zeus by capturing his progeny. He sent me to find you and your sisters, and to warn you."

She jumped up off the couch. "My sisters? You've found them?"

He shook his head again. "No, not yet. You are the only one I've tracked down so far, but I have some ideas about the others."

She touched his hand. "You must find them. I'm fine here, please go and warn my sisters."

"Oh. My. Goddess. You really *have* changed. But I can't do that. Zeus would have my head. Trouble has already found you and I fear the rebels have already arrived. Once you are safe I'll find them, I promise."

"Thank you. I'll keep you to that." Corey sank back on the couch, slowly blowing out a breath. "And yes, there have been a few strange happenings over the last couple of days."

"Almost being run down in the street wasn't the first?"

She pointed toward the ceiling. "I found a doll that looked suspiciously like me hanging from those rafters last night."

Eros grimaced. "That's just sick."

"And there's that small legal problem I had yesterday. But James got me out of that one."

"He's a lawyer?"

"They call them solicitors here in Sydney."

"Solicitor then. Whatever you call them, you can't trust them."

A loud knock sounded at the front door. She flinched as the sound got louder.

"Would you like me to see who that is?" Eros asked.

"Corey? Open the door for God's sake."

Her eyes widened. "James?"

Eros smiled. "I guess that answers that question. Shall I let him in?"

Her shoulders slumped. "No, I'll get it. He can't see you."

"What? I'm being pushed aside?" He placed his hand over his heart in a mock act of being wounded.

She shooed him away with her hands. "Eros, please. We can talk later."

The door shook and the screws in the hinges were working themselves out. She zapped them with her eyes to retighten them. When she looked back, Eros had disappeared.

She opened the door to a disheveled-looking James, his hand poised to do further damage to the poor timber. "There's no need to destroy my property, James."

"Corey. Thank God you're all right."

What is he doing here? The compulsion should still be working. "Of course I'm all right. Why wouldn't I be?"

"Can I come in?"

She turned on her heel and walked toward the sitting area. "So what's with the pounding on the door? Did you leave your personal organizer here last night and discover you can't get through the day without it?" *Why did I say that? I sound like the bitch I used to be.*

James came up behind and wrapped his arms around her, resting his chin on her head. His comforting warmth seeped into her tense muscles. "I came as soon as I heard. Are you okay?"

She stiffened. How did he know about the car? She didn't call the police. Only George knew. "What are you talking about?"

He released her and turned her around. "The car that almost ran you down. I had to make sure you were okay."

"How did you find out about that? It only happened half an hour ago, and I haven't spoken to anyone about it." Except for Eros, but he didn't need to know that.

His eyes narrowed. "I was worried about you, so I asked a friend to keep an eye on you."

Really? Her heart did a little happy dance, but she wasn't letting him off the hook yet. "You've got a funny way of showing it. You left this morning without so much as a goodbye."

He had the grace to look embarrassed. "Sorry about that. I had an early morning meeting and didn't have the heart to wake you."

"You mean you didn't want to deal with the awkwardness."

"Not exactly."

It was probably not a good idea to continue that conversation, so instead she walked into the kitchen and poured a glass of water. "You have someone spying on me?"

James followed her, invading her personal space and preventing her from leaving. "Someone is threatening you, Corey. We may have only just met, but that doesn't mean I don't care about what happens to you."

"After last night, I thought we knew each other rather well, actually."

Heat flared in his eyes. "We had great sex, but we hardly know anything about each other."

Her heart stopped for a few seconds as the air whooshed out of her lungs. *Great sex?* The guy had a serious case of denial. His presence here proved that.

"Keep telling yourself that and we both might believe it one day."

"Corey—"

"Don't worry. I'm still trying to get over the fact that you put someone on my tail." "So where is he? Or is it a she? "She moved to the front window, and opened the curtains. "Is it that blue Corolla? The green Holden?"

James crossed the room and drew the curtains back in place. "Don't make yourself a target, Corey. You have to be careful." He slid his arm around her shoulders and steered them both toward the couch and sat her down next to him. "This is serious. Someone is trying to kill you. We need to call the police."

"No." How could she explain the Titan rebels? He wouldn't believe her. *No one would believe me.* She sighed, and shrugged her shoulders. "It's probably just a series of coincidences. Why would anyone want to kill me?"

He narrowed his eyes. "You tell me."

Thank the goddess one of her talents was acting, because the innocent laugh she gave would have won her an Oscar. "No one wants to kill me, I have no enemies. I'm just a dancer." She could have sworn she heard someone coughing in the background. *Be quiet, Eros!*

"I don't see any harm in getting the police to investigate."

"You wouldn't say that if you were in my position. Remember, only a few days ago they were happy to believe I was a prostitute. As if they're going to take this seriously!"

James sat back against the couch and crossed his arms. "Fine. I'll do some investigating myself. I'm not without my own resources."

Her heart started pitter-pattering all over the place. *Oh wow. He really does care about me.* Maybe her plan would work after all? But she didn't want him to put himself in danger—he had no idea what he was up against. It would take all her and Eros' considerable powers just to keep themselves safe, let alone keep a mortal out of harm's way. No, she couldn't let him be involved in this.

Standing up, she walked back to the kitchen bench and picked up her glass of water. "I appreciate the thought, but really, it's not necessary. I'm quite capable of looking after myself."

He stood and followed her into the kitchen. "I'm sure you are, but get used to me hanging around. I have no intention of leaving you alone until we get this thing worked out."

She raised her glass to her lips and sipped the cool water. "What about the person you have spying on me?"

"An ex-cop who owed me a favor. He's been keeping an eye on you since this morning. It's that mannequin that has me worried. The person behind that has a very sick mind. Are you sure there isn't some old boyfriend out there?"

She turned away, her head down. "No. No old boyfriends. I haven't had time since I came to Sydney. I've been too busy getting my dance studio established." *Not like my old life when men idolized me and it was party, party, party all the time.*

"What about the dancing at The Cave?"

"I do that for my own pleasure. It's a casual arrangement I have with the manager. Whenever the mood takes me, I just show up."

"None of the patrons have become a nuisance? Followed you home?"

"No one, until that spoiled brat the other day."

"Either way, I want you to come and stay with me until we work out what's happening."

The mouthful of water she'd just sipped sprayed out and dribbled down her face. She ripped a few sheets of paper towel off the bench, then patted her mouth and the front of her shirt in between coughs. "You're kidding, right?"

"I never kid."

No way. She couldn't put him in danger that way. Now she knew who she was up against, it didn't matter that she wanted to be with him, his safety was the priority now. There was no way she could let him get involved.

"I'm sorry, James, but I can't do that. I have a business to run and you have a law practice. Neither of us can afford to put everything on hold. It's completely out of the question."

She had tried dealing with her problems without magic. However, now she had her powers back it was time to use them. James would be pissed off if he knew she was doing this, but there wasn't any other way she could see to keep him safe. She closed her eyes and concentrated. *You will trust Corey to look after herself.*

With a puzzled look on his face James slowly walked away, his voice a flat monotone when he spoke. "I suppose I should trust you to look after yourself."

Good. It's working.

She opened the door and gestured for him to go. *You will leave now, and you will go back to your office.*

James slowly ambled out as if reluctant to go, but finding no reason to stay. "I guess I should get back to work. I left in the middle of an important meeting."

He did? "Thanks for coming over, James. As you can see, I'm fine. It was just a freak accident." *Don't phone Corey because you will be too busy for at least the next two weeks.*

"I'll give you a call sometime."

Corey plastered a smile on her face, even though she ached at the possibility of never seeing him again. Whatever the outcome, he was inside her soul now and no one would ever take his place. "Sure thing."

She stepped back and grasped the door handle. The gentle touch of his hand on her shoulder stopped her in her tracks.

"I can't leave without first doing this." He cupped her face and kissed her. Smiling, he pulled back and turned away, walking toward his car. Corey touched her tingling lips as she watched him drive away, one small tear sliding down her cheek. *Please stay safe.*

Chapter Four

The phone rang as James entered his office. He cursed, hoping like hell it wasn't anything important. He had a mountain of work to catch up on, so why the fuck did he spend so much time worrying about Corey? She'd been around the traps. She knew the score and how to look after herself. She certainly didn't need him.

He threw his mobile phone down on the partners' desk and sat down before snatching the desk phone from its cradle. "Barrington."

"Jimmy boy, I've been trying to find you."

"Dave. I'm glad you called. I was just about to call you."

"Glad I saved you the trouble. I wanted to bring you up to speed with the investigation."

"You didn't find anything, did you? I thought as—"

Dave cut him off. "No, that isn't it. I've got a lead on the car that almost ran your girlfriend down."

"Don't worry about it, Dave. It was just a coincidence. Must have been a kid joyriding."

"No, I don't think so."

"Had to be. It was some kid in a stolen car, not used to driving, and the car got out of control."

"Nup. It's not that. Your girlfriend is obviously a deliberate target."

James stood up, his grip on the phone tightening. "What do you mean?"

"We found the car abandoned."

"So?"

"It had a picture of your girlfriend in it, with her studio address on the back. It was definitely no accident."

Running his fingers through his hair, he moved back to the desk. "So have you questioned any witnesses? Do you have her under surveillance?"

"We would if we could find her."

It took a few seconds for the implication to sink in. A strong belief of how it was all a coincidence warred with his natural instincts to protect her, and the persistent gut feeling that something was very wrong. His brain hurt and the urge to throw up increased with every passing second. The gut feeling won. She was in danger and he'd left her alone, unguarded.

Idiot!

"Fuck. You lost her? Bloody great detectives you are. Shit!"

"Fair go, mate. A minute ago you told me to drop the whole thing. After you arrived at her studio, I figured she was safe for a while, so I went back to the station and started tracking down the car. I got half of the plate from the coffee shop owner, plus he was pretty sure of the make and model, so it wasn't long before we found the car. By the time we found the evidence and went back to question her, she'd gone."

What had possessed me to leave her? "Did you try her home?"

"Well, duh. Of course we did. She wasn't there either. I thought she might be with you."

She should be with me, but I left her alone.

"I left her half an hour ago. She was fine."

"And you have no idea where she might be?"

He had an idea, but after this stuff-up, there was no way he wasn't getting involved himself. "No, not really. I don't know her very well."

A loud snort sounded through the handset. "Yeah, right. Like you two haven't been fucking ever since you met."

"I'm her solicitor, Dave." Although this was true, why did he feel it was hell of a lot more than that?

"Like that's going to stop you."

Ignoring the ribbing he slipped his keys back in his pocket and picked up his mobile. "You'd better get moving on finding her. I'll let you know if I hear anything, and I expect you to do the same."

"Bloody hell, James. You have to give me more to work with. You must have some idea where she might have gone."

"No, but I'll let you know if I find anything. Thanks for calling, Davo. I owe you one."

"And I plan on collecting big time."

"You do that." His brain worked overtime as he carelessly dropped the handset back into the cradle of the console.

His mind replayed the last twenty-four hours. A mutilated effigy of Corey had been found hanging from her rafters. He'd humored her by taking her out to dinner instead of doing what his first instinct had told him to do, and reporting it to the police. They'd had amazing sex, then he'd pulled back and left without even saying goodbye. Today someone had tried to run her down, and he'd turned up guns blazing, trying to tell her what to do.

She must hate his guts. *Jeezus,* he hated himself.

He didn't understand that abrupt turnabout where he'd gone and left her unprotected. He searched his mind for a clue as to what had happened. He knew without a doubt that he'd gone there determined to whisk her off somewhere safe until the police had found whoever was doing this but something had happened to make him change his mind. There was no way he would have done that willingly. *How did she do it?* Come to think of it, what had made him go there the night before? Nothing made sense from the minute he'd met that woman, but by God, he'd never felt more alive, or, as of this moment, more scared shitless.

* * * *

The Cave was not exactly what he had expected. Plush, velvet seats lined booths situated against the walls, and chairs in the front of the stage barricaded by a wrought iron railing. The stage was set well back from the patrons, and although the dancers weren't completely nude, a couple of them had strategically placed patches of sequins that left absolutely nothing to the imagination.

James scanned the dimly lit room and zeroed in on a raised cage to one side. The height of the platform made it impossible for anyone to reach the dancer moving and sliding up against the shimmering pole at the center. Cigar smoke irritated his nose as he strode across the room hoping it was Corey up in that cage. It was as she'd described to him, right down to the height of the cage above the audience. Seductive music pounded out of speakers that surrounded the room, adding to the deafening thump of a subwoofer. His pulse nervously thrummed in time to the rhythm. Edging closer, he stared at the blonde woman with the sexy, supple body moving to the music, circling her long, shapely legs around the pole above the crowd. There was no mistaking that body, she was magnificent. Sensuality oozed from every pore of her satiny skin. Somehow, she had managed to take a raw and basic dance and turn it into an artistic masterpiece. His dick hardened, proving that where Corey was concerned, he had little control. The chemistry between them was too strong, like an invisible thread reeling him in, little by little.

Leaning against the wall, he contented himself by watching her until the dance was over. He might as well enjoy the view while he could. She'd be finished in a few minutes, and he intended to move her to a safe place. This time he wouldn't let whatever mind games she used dissuade him from his purpose. Nothing short of a nuclear explosion would stop him from keeping her safe this time.

The music faded before he could approach the platform and he watched Corey climb down the iron stairs at the rear of the cage and disappear behind the velvet curtains that separated the performers from the audience. Picking up speed, he jumped the iron railing, then threw open the curtains as he reached the backstage area. The bright lights contrasted with the dimness of the club and it took a few seconds for his eyes to adjust. A series of doors lined the corridor, which led to the rear of the club. He opened the first one, but one of the muscle shirt-clad bouncers stood in his way, an immovable object the size of half a mountain.

"Get the fuck out of here, shithead. This is a private dressing room," he said.

Trying to look past the giant in front of him, James raised his voice as the music resumed. "I'm looking for Corey. I need to speak to her urgently."

"You and every other randy dude in town. Now piss off."

"I'm afraid I must insist. It's a matter of life and death."

"Oh yeah, that's what they all say." The giant placed his enormous hands against his chest and pushed, effortlessly shoving James across to the opposite wall as the door slammed in front of him.

He jumped up and pounded. "Hey, I have to speak to Corey. Now! It's really important."

Realizing he wouldn't find her that way he looked around and decided to check out the other rooms. However, before he could even take one step, two more bouncers arrived and headed right for him.

Fuck!

Retreat seemed like the best course of action at this stage, so he backed up and headed into the club. There had to be another way to get past the muscle and find Corey. As he headed for the front door, he pulled his phone out of his pocket and tried Corey's phone again, only to shove it back when she still didn't pick up.

After leaving through the front of the club, he scouted the laneway. He screwed up his nose, trying to mask the disgusting odors wafting about. The garbage containers reeked of rotting food and excrement and he struggled not to throw up. He found the gate at the end of the alley locked, but it opened readily enough with a shove from his shoulder. The back door of the club was in his sights when a young woman ran out of the building in obvious distress.

James sprinted across the space, catching up with her as she tried to run toward the main street. She screamed as he closed the distance and caught up with her.

"Get away from me."

He held onto her arm as she struggled to get away. "Hey, I'm not going to hurt you. I just want to ask you some questions."

"Get real," she said as she pushed his hand off. "I just want to get the fuck out of here. Let me go."

"Please, just one question and I'll leave you alone," he said, stepping back and giving the girl some space. "I'm looking for Corey. Is she still inside?"

The girl paled, her hands shaking as she picked at a piece of fluff on her coat.

"Please, you have to tell me if you know anything. I have to find her, she's in danger."

The girl lowered her head and stared at her feet. "It may be too late. He took her."

What? No!

Her words were like a kick in the guts, pushing all the air out of his lungs so he could only manage a whisper. "Who took her?" He gripped her chin, raising her face. "What are you talking about?"

Shaking her head, she tried to wriggle away, but he held fast.

"Where is she?"

A tiny tear trickled down the girl's cheeks. "This old dude was waiting for her in her dressing room. I heard her yelling at him to go back to the hellhole he came from, but he just laughed at her."

"What happened after that?"

She shifted from one foot to another. "If I tell you, you'll think I'm crazy."

"Just tell me for God's sake."

"It sounded like a storm, with the wind howling, and then it went quiet. I looked in to see if Corey was okay, but she was gone and the room was trashed. I know she didn't leave through the door because she would have passed me."

Holy shit. He knew weird stuff was happening around Corey, but this was unbelievable. "Is there a window?"

"You see that's the thing. The windows are boarded up. There is no way to get out of that room except the door. You probably think I'm mad. But I'm not."

She wrenched herself free of his grasp and started to run off. "I'm outta here. This is just too weird."

His mind was in turmoil as she ran down the street. He slipped back inside, careful to avoid the bouncers, and found the room exactly as the girl had described. Upturned chairs, makeup and clothing strewn from one end of the room to the other. The shattered mirror left dozens of shards scattered all over the floor. Scanning the walls, he noted the wood blocking the windows and saw no visible means of escape. *So what the fuck happened?* He smashed his fist against the wall, before walking back to his car to regroup. Maybe Davo would have some ideas, because he sure as hell had run out.

* * * *

Corey woke slowly, her head throbbing like a symphony of drums. Forcing her eyes open, she groaned. Her nostrils twitched as the dank smell of sulfur overwhelmed her.

Oh goddess, no!

Her memory came back with a vengeance and she slumped back against the cold rock. Prometheus, the Titan traitor, had brought her here—the Underworld. How the heck would she escape? With all her heart she wished herself back with James. He was her destiny, but a side trip to hell made fulfilling it a tad difficult.

She hugged her knees close to her chest as the cold seeped into her bones. Her powers were useless here, so gaining her freedom meant she would have to rely on her wits and determination. Given that only mortals could escape the Underworld, her chances of achieving that were rather slim.

A tear slid down her cheek as she thought of how she might never see James again. As a goddess, she took what people gave her without further thought, but James had taught her that giving of yourself was many times more rewarding. Never had she dreamed that the concept of giving one's self—one's soul—to a person could ever be a sane and logical thing to do. Until James, she'd never really understood why mortals left themselves open to the intense, emotional pain of unconditional love. But she was coming to the conclusion that the risk was worth it. She vowed to give more of herself if she ever got the chance again. She'd already given her heart to James, and if she never escaped, at least she had a beautiful memory.

A flash of light pulled her back to the present as her enemy materialized. He had always had a flair for the dramatic, but no one ever took him seriously. He definitely had her attention now.

"Prometheus. I could say I'm glad to see you, but that would be a lie."

His laugh made her cringe. "Terpsichore, I am immune to your insults. I stopped listening to your meaningless prattle eons ago."

She stood up and crossed her arms as she walked away and showed him her back.

"Fine. Send me back home then."

She sensed him staring at her, but there was no way she would turn around and give him the satisfaction of seeing how much he rattled her.

"Revenge is sweet, my dear. Your dear father deserves to feel maximum pain."

She grimaced and faked a laugh. "Haven't you heard? I've been banished by my father's wife. There is no revenge in harming me."

"That may be true, but Zeus would never allow others to take what he considers his own. When he hears of my plans for his daughters, he will fall for my trap and I will finally have my revenge. Bringing you here to the place of my incarceration is merely the first step.

She swung around to face him, her fists clenched. "So why did you bring me here? Why all the tricks? You could have killed me in my home."

"That would have been too easy," he sneered. "I wanted you off balance, to suffer... And yes, I could have killed you there in that strange place, and indeed I plan to eventually, but not until after I have you and your sisters together. When I have captured all of the Muses your father will be more than willing to negotiate for your release."

This time she laughed for real. "You don't know Zeus if you think he will bargain with you. He never negotiates. He will hunt you down and destroy you."

"Oh no, not this time... Not when I have his precious daughters. He will do anything to get them back, and thus I will have my revenge." He waved his hand in a circle, cutting through the steamy air. "Enough. I have plans to make. I trust you will enjoy my accommodations."

"Wait. I need food and drink. You can't get your revenge if I am dead before you finish."

"Fine." He snapped his fingers and a tray of food and wine appeared on the floor. "Enjoy it while it lasts, Terpsichore. I will be back." Waving his arm, he disappeared in a haze of smoke.

Dejected, she ignored the food and slumped back down to the floor. She feared for her sisters, and her heart ached from the loss of James. Who would help her in this horrible place? *Who knows I'm here?*

Of course! She straightened up, feeling hopeful for the first time since she had woken up in this godforsaken place. *Eros!* She prayed to the gods that he had been watching her closely. If anyone could figure out a way to help her, he could.

* * * *

After checking the dance studio, James made his way to Corey's house. He was desperate to pick up her trail and was fast running out of ideas. After she'd disappeared from the club, he'd called Dave. The cop had taken the situation very seriously, and that more than anything had scared the shit out of him. Okay, Dave didn't actually believe the bit about her disappearing into thin air, but James was ready to believe anything at this point. Since he'd met Corey, weird stuff had happened to the point where even he was acting completely out of character. Losing control wasn't his usual way and while his head told him he didn't need her in his nice, neat, orderly life, his heart wasn't listening. The thought of never seeing her again and never holding her in his arms was like a fist in his gut.

He parked his car on the verge in front of her home, then jumped out and sprinted to the front door. As he raised his fist to knock, the door opened to reveal a man—a good-looking, blond giant of a man who grabbed his hand and drew him inside.

"Good, you're here. We don't have much time. Let's go."

"Who the fuck are you?"

The giant sighed. "That's not important right now, we need to get moving. Corey is in trouble and only you can help her."

James turned around to face him and stood his ground. "What the hell are you talking about? How am I the only one who can help her?"

He blew out a dramatic sigh. "I guess you had to be told sooner or later."

"Told what?"

"You're the only one who can help Terpsichore because you are mortal."

"Come again?" *What the fuck is he talking about?*

"It really is very simple. You are mortal. Corey and I are not."

James swiveled his head, looking around him from side to side. "Is there a hidden camera somewhere? Is this some sort of joke?"

"No joke, my friend, but like I said—we don't have time for this. I thought about easing you into it, but the quicker we get to Corey, the better. Hold onto my arm and close your eyes."

"What?"

"I forgot. You mortals can never see past the end of your nose. Never mind, here we go." He grabbed hold of James' wrist and waved his arm back and forth.

The earth spun as they were pulled into some sort of vortex.

Holy shit!

Several minutes and a couple of dizzy spells later, the spinning stopped. James opened and closed his eyes a few times to clear his vision. He could have sworn he was in a dark cave, but that had to be his imagination. Before he closed his eyes he'd been standing outside Corey's house.

"Open your eyes, mortal."

"You say *mortal* as if it's an insult," he said as he blinked the last few times as the dizziness subsided. "What the heck was that mind trip we just went on...?" They really were in a cave. "Oh. Shit."

The smell hit him first, reminiscent of the sulfur gas of hot springs. Steam swirled around, obscuring visibility. While his eyes registered what he saw, his mind denied it. It couldn't be happening. His crazy companion must have jabbed him with a hallucinogen when he'd grabbed him. It was the only explanation for this freaky nightmare. He closed his eyes and screwed them shut.

I'll close my eyes and when I open them again, all will be back to normal.

He pried open one eye. *Damn, it didn't work. I'm still here.*

"Okay, mate. What you said about you and Corey not being mortal—I think I'm ready to hear it now."

The blond picked himself up off the floor of the cave where the force of the whirlwind had thrown him. "I'll give you the short version. If we are successful, there will be time for long explanations later."

"Fine. Hurry up so we can get Corey and go back home."

"All righty then. Have you knowledge of Greek mythology?"

"I remember a little from ancient history class. Hang on," he said, "Terpsichore is one of the Muses, isn't she?" He ran his hand through his hair as he paced across the floor. "But she can't be the same one. The Muses are a myth."

"Oh, but she is. She is Terpsichore, the Muse of Dance and daughter of Zeus and Mnemosyne. And no, we are not myths."

"Freaking hell." He'd fallen for a goddess. *Holy shit – a goddess!*

"So who are you then? Apollo?"

The giant snorted. "No, I am not. I am Eros."

James laughed. "Where's your bow and arrow?"

"That is just a vicious story put around by my enemies to reduce my credibility. I do not shoot arrows and I do not walk around half dressed." He smiled wickedly. "Well, not all the time."

Now he knew what Alice had felt like when she'd fallen down the rabbit hole. "So where are we? This doesn't look like any description I've ever read about Olympus."

Eros walked around the cave, inspecting the walls as he moved. "That's because it's not. This is the Underworld."

"The Underworld? You mean *Hades*?"

"The Palace of Hades is but a small part of the Underworld. There are also the Elysian Fields, the Plain of Judgment, the Vale of Mourning, and many more."

"So what part are we in?"

"I can't be exactly sure, but from the look of the walls here in the cave, we're near the rock in the center of the Underworld. Corey must be very close, I can feel her."

He couldn't believe he was doing this, but he asked the question anyway. "You said I was the only one who could help Corey. Tell me what I need to do."

Eros stopped pacing. "Because you are mortal, we will be able to return with you to the surface. It is your mortality that allows this. As long as we touch through the portal at Troezen, we can go through."

His eyes narrowed. "How do you know it will work?"

"Because it's worked before. Dionysus brought his mother back, and Heracles returned, bringing with him the hound of Hades."

"That makes me feel so much better. How can I fail? Mythical characters came before me."

"I repeat. They are not mythical."

"Considering your name is Eros, and I'm standing here with you, I guess not. What's the plan?"

Eros rolled his eyes. "First we must find Corey. We must be careful since these caves have many tunnels and we can easily get lost."

"Can't you just wave your arms and poof, we're there?"

Eros shook his head. "My powers do not work here."

"So how did Corey get here if the magic powers don't work?

Eros shrugged. "They are not magic powers, mortal, and I have no idea. The monster who did this had his taken away from him. He must have gained the assistance of one of the gods of the Underworld. When

Zeus finds out he's going to be beyond angry. He doesn't deal well with traitors."

James nodded his head. "Great. Good to know. I'll make sure I don't piss off Zeus. I guess we'll try and use stealth and intelligence instead. At least you look like you'd be good in a fight. I'm not so sure I'll be that much help. I flunked self-defense class."

Snickering, Eros headed for the mouth of the cave. "Never fear, mortal. Besides my romantic side, I am known for my physical strength."

"I must have missed that one," he murmured.

"What did you say, mortal?"

"Nothing."

The two men walked together out of the cave, the light outside marginally better. James surveyed the dark and desolate landscape. The trees in the distance bore no greenery, and the large branches looked like large claws reaching out to whoever walked beneath them. The path in front of them led into the trees, and toward bare plains covered with mist. He closed his eyes, still incredulous that he was here, walking through the Underworld, and that the woman of his dreams was a goddess. He expected to wake up at any minute. The heat and the odor of sulfur reminded him that this was a new reality, so he'd better get used to it.

Drawing deep inside himself, he tried to picture Corey in his mind. The memories of all the encounters they'd had flashed in front of his eyes. Was it only a few days ago? From that first meeting at the police station, the spark had been there. From that moment on, his life had changed.

"Mortal?"

He opened his eyes. "What?"

"We must hurry. Can you feel her?"

Surprised that Eros could read his thoughts so easily, he frowned. "Yes, I can, but I have no idea what direction to take."

"We can only find out if we try." He pointed toward the trees. "This way first. It offers us the best cover from the evil that surrounds us."

Heading down the path, James voiced another question. "Speaking of evil, who is this guy who brought Corey here, and what does he want with her?"

"Prometheus, a traitor to Olympus. He was banished by Zeus, so he plots his revenge by taking from Zeus what is his. What I don't understand is how he is using his powers. They removed them when he was banished, but somehow he can move around the dimensions."

"So how can we elude this Prometheus character?"

"He will not be expecting us, so we have surprise on our side. We must make sure we are not detected."

"What can he do to us?"

"He can make sure we never leave here."

Oh great. "Then we'd better be very careful. There's no way I'm staying in this horrible place. It's giving me the creeps."

* * * *

The messenger bowed low as he entered the sacred chamber and awaited the bidding of his master, Zeus, King of the Ancient World.

"What news do you bring of my daughters?"

Edging forward, the soldier raised his head and directed his gaze at his King. "Your greatness, we have word that Prometheus has captured Terpsichore and imprisoned her in the Underworld."

"He dares interfere with my family?" Zeus rose from his place, gesturing for the others in the room to leave. "We must rescue her. How can he be doing this?" Zeus paced back and forth, as he pumped and tapped his fists against his thighs before snatching a goblet from the table. "He must have used ancient magic to regain his powers. Either that or we have a traitor in our ranks."

The goblet in his hand smashed against the marble floor, spilling the golden liquid in rivulets across the room.

The messenger stepped back, avoiding the trail of liquid. "All may not be lost, my lord. Eros has enlisted the help of a mortal and is in the Underworld as we speak."

Zeus stopped pacing and smiled. "Excellent. The traitor will not expect that. Send a garrison to Troezen to guard the portal. They will need assistance on their return."

Bowing as he backed away, the soldier nodded. "As you wish, my lord."

Zeus moved to the window and glanced across the courtyard to where his wife sat with her ladies-in-waiting. "You haven't won this round, Hera. Terpsichore will soon be back amongst us, as will all of Mnemosyne's daughters. Your jealousy shall not prevail."

Hera raised her head, catching sight of her husband. She smiled and raised her goblet in salute.

He did not respond. *Not this time. Her time will come.*

* * * *

Corey explored the cave, desperate to find an escape route. She gingerly rubbed her hand where she'd been zapped by a wall of enchantment at the entrance, designed to prevent her from leaving. The sensation of hundreds of tiny pinpricks darted through her burning fingertips. No point in trying that way again.

Although she didn't really believe she would find a way out through the back of the cave. Prometheus would not imprison her in a place that had even the smallest chance of escape — but she still had to give it a try. He might have missed something.

Unease crawled under her skin like ants. She held her breath and stopped dead in her tracks. Someone was here with her — she could sense it. Slowly she turned her head, scanning the area. She heard a shuffling sound near the back of the cave. On full alert, she silently moved toward the direction of the noise.

Thud.

She heard it again, barely discernible, but there all the same. She moved over to the wall and inched slowly toward a dark hole. Although she was certain she'd already checked this part of the cave, now she wasn't so sure. Her pulse kicked up the decibels inside her head, blocking out all other sound. When she reached the black hole, she stopped, willing her heartbeat to slow down. With every breath she took, she deepened her inhalation and slowly exhaled until she could feel herself calming down.

Bracing herself for a quick escape, she peered around the corner and into the darkness. It took a few minutes for her eyes to adjust.

She saw a few dark and uneven shapes, but it was difficult to discern anything at all as nothing was moving. Cocking her ear, she waited for another sound that would give her a hint as to what was there. She wiped her hand across her forehead, pushing the sweat out of her eyes. She heard a shuffle again. It was farther in the distance than before, so she followed the sound along the passageway.

The darkness was less oppressive the farther she walked, becoming lighter as she moved. The path twisted and turned until finally she came to a dead end. At least it appeared like a dead end, until she touched the wall.

"Ouch."

She jerked her arm back. Sparks of electrical activity jumped off the wall and revealed the outside of the cave. When she withdrew her hand, the illusion of rock returned. *Strange.* It must be an enchanted portal. *How did one get through?* Her hand still burnt from the brief touch and she feared she wouldn't be able to make it through safely. Perhaps there was a way to disable it. A sound startled her and she jumped back, catching her elbow on the rock behind and sending a shooting pain up her arm. "Argh."

The wall buzzed and hissed, then a small furry creature ran through the portal, apparently unharmed. That must have been what she'd heard. She could see the outside of the cave as the rodent passed through. Maybe if she threw something across the portal it would give her enough time to pass through herself.

It was certainly worth a try.

She crouched down and swept her hands over the floor, looking for a loose object. Against the wall she found a piece of rock about the size of a grapefruit. She held it between both her hands and stood up. The cold, uneven surface lay heavy in her palms. Would it work, or was she throwing herself into more danger?

What choice do I have?

Even if escaping the Underworld was not possible, at least she would be free of Prometheus. Taking a deep breath, she readied herself to sprint through the portal as soon the rock went through. One, two, three… She threw the rock, leaping nanoseconds after the throw.

Right into a hard body.

Holy Olympus! She tried to escape but steely arms wrapped around her, drawing her closer to the hard, muscular form.

"Corey?"

She looked up and her heart leaped. "James? Oh my goddess, James. It's really you?"

His arms tightened further. "Eros told me you were in danger, which is why he brought me here. Thank God we found you."

"We?"

"Hello there, my little Muse."

Twisting in James' arms, she spied her other rescuer. "Eros. Thank the gods you paid attention. How did you know where to find me?"

"This is the only place Prometheus is welcome these days. It was logical to assume he would be where he is safe from the wrath of Zeus."

She moved out of James' arms and hugged her friend. "Thank you, Erie. My father will reward you."

"Speaking of your father, there seem to be a few things you've forgotten to tell me," said James.

Tensing, she turned back to face him, searching his face for signs of anger, but found only curiosity. Her shoulders relaxed and she took his hand. "You already thought I was a weirdo, would you have believed me?"

He smiled and her heart turned over.

He squeezed her hand. "Probably not. But when we get the time, I want to hear the whole story. Right now, we need to get out of this place."

Eros signaled them to be quiet. Someone was approaching from farther down the path. James pulled her with him and they crouched behind a large rock.

"Who is it?" Corey whispered.

Eros closed his eyes and breathed in the scents around them. "It's not Prometheus, but we can't take any chances. It could be one of his soldiers."

After the dark figure had passed them by, and continued down the path without stopping, they all relaxed.

"So what's the plan?" asked James, pulling Corey closer to his side. She held his hand and he rubbed her palm with his thumb, sending warm fuzzies all through her body.

"We must find the portal for the exit at Troezen. Zeus will be waiting for us on the other side."

"He will?" said James and Corey in unison.

"I dispatched a message to him before I brought James here. He is aware of where we are and who is responsible."

"That is good news, Eros, but how do we find the portal?"

"Never fear. Heracles and I had this long drinking session several years back, and he may have let a few secrets slip. I think I know exactly where we need to be."

James stood up, helping Corey to her feet. "So what are we waiting for? Let's get the hell out of here."

"I said I might know where we need to be. I didn't say I know how to get there."

Corey smiled at his obscure statement. He hadn't changed. "Stop playing word games, Erie. You have a pretty good idea, don't you?"

His lips twitched with mischief. "Maybe... Maybe not."

James bristled and his grip on Corey's hand increased. "This is not a game. We need to get out of here. Now, do you know where to go or don't you?"

"All right, I have an idea of where we need to go."

"Then lead on. I want to get back home."

Corey sighed. Did he want to go to her home, or his? With or without her? The grip of his hand was reassuring, but could he handle the truth that was Olympus?

She shrugged and realized both men were waiting for her. "What?"

"We're moving on. Are you ready?"

"Ready as I'll ever be."

* * * *

They stopped to rest a few hours later. Eros shared his wineskin between the three of them, although there wasn't a lot left. They needed to find water soon, but Eros warned that the water from the rivers in the Underworld contained magic, so they had to be careful. James and Eros hardly seemed out of breath, but Corey was exhausted. Although physically fit from her dancing, the last few days had taken their toll. If she sat down for too long, she knew she would not be able to stand up and get moving again.

"How much longer until we reach this place?" asked James.

"I can see the Palace of Hades in the distance now. It is very near."

Dragging herself to her feet, Corey groaned. "I hope we can avoid Cerberus. Our powers do not work here—it took the strength of Heracles to subdue him in the past."

"Cerberus? The three-headed dog? Oh great. This is becoming more and more like a sappy episode from *Hercules*."

Eros narrowed his eyes. "That production bears no resemblance to the truth."

"I hope not, but from what I've read about Hades' dog, we might be in big trouble here"

Placing her hand on James' forearm, she reassured him. "We will avoid the dog—" She looked over her shoulder at Eros. "Won't we?"

"Of course. No one in their right mind aggravates Cerberus. As you mortals say...a piece of cake."

A roar of mammoth proportions filled the air and the ground shook beneath their feet.

James spun around, his eyes darting from side to side, scanning the fields that surrounded them. "Fuck! What was that?"

"Um...that would be Cerberus," said Eros.

James stopped walking. "Shit. How do we get past him?"

"We don't need to." Eros led them to a large rock at the side of the pathway. "Help me move this, James. If memory serves correctly, the portal lies on the other side."

"How do you know this is the right place?" James asked.

Eros pointed to the rock where some symbols had been scratched. "Heracles told me about some markings near the ground, and this is the only rock I see here with anything like what he described."

Corey moved to the side of the rock and braced her hands against it. "Come on then, let's do it."

All three of them pushed and shoved, working up lots of sweat and producing much colorful language. It took all of their combined strength to do it, but finally the rock shifted and a large dark hole appeared behind it. James removed a flaming torch from the wall beside them and flashed it across the opening, revealing a staircase hewn into the rock that led upwards through the mountainside.

James patted Eros on the back. "It looks like we lucked out. Let's get moving before that creature gets us."

"Not so fast, Terpsichore."

Oh no! James pushed Corey behind him, shielding her from the man who threatened her.

"Prometheus, I presume."

Corey touched his arm as soldiers surrounded them, blocking their escape. "James, be careful."

Prometheus smiled, his cruel face lined with age. "My, my, my, the mortal has some fire. Who would have thought?"

Corey came out from behind James and stood tall. "Let them go, Prometheus. I'll do whatever you ask."

He snickered. "You must think me an idiot, Terpsichore. Why would I let them go and allow that mortal to get to your father? You all stay."

He turned to the soldiers and nodded. "Take them to the caves and this time tie them up."

"What harm can a mere mortal do? Let him go!"

Prometheus turned back to her. "Nice try, but I know better. He means something to you so I'm keeping him. Eros, however, is just an annoying git and locking him away will be a great pleasure."

"Huh! I am deeply offended by that remark." Eros took a step toward Prometheus before being hurled back by two of the soldiers.

"Enough of this nonsense," bellowed Prometheus. "Take them away!"

* * * *

Terpsichore rubbed her temple as she sat on the cold, hard floor of the cave. At least the ties on her wrists allowed her to do that. Her feet were losing feeling, and so was her behind as she sat there. It had been a long night and none of them had gotten much sleep. After the obligatory attempt to wriggle out of the ropes, they'd all given up and taken turns to doze. Beside her James lay against the wall, his face deep in thought. She was racked with guilt for dragging him into this. If they ever got out of here she would spend the rest of her life making it up to him. He turned and smiled at her as she took her hands away from her face.

"How can you be smiling at a time like this?"

"I was remembering a scene in *Xena* where Zena and Gabrielle were trapped in a cave, not unlike this one."

Eros snorted. "You actually watched that ridiculous show? *Hercules* was bad enough…"

"I might have caught one or two episodes. It was a long time ago now. It was research," said James, laughing.

"Ha… I bet it was the girl on girl action."

It was James' turn to snort now. "Maybe it was, but they escaped a lot of places just like this. I say we try some of their tactics."

Corey smiled at both of them while they discussed tactics. She sat up straight as she listened. This was getting interesting. "You know, guys, this might just work!"

Eros huffed at her. "Of course it will work. My plans always work."

"Oh really? I can remember that time…"

"Never mind. Okay, not always, but this one will!"

"Shh, folks. We don't want the guards to hear us!"

"He's right. Let's keep the noise down and go over it a few more times so we're all on the same page."

An hour later they'd agreed on an escape plan, but as they needed to wait for an opportunity they decided to fill in the time getting the kinks out of their muscles.

Corey rocked forward on her ankles until she gained her footing and pushed down, thrusting her body upwards. Sometimes she was so glad she was a dancer. Her leg muscles burned, but the effort to stand wasn't too bad. She wasn't sure how James and Eros were doing. James at least had the advantage, being a mortal used to doing things for himself. Eros, on the other hand, usually waved his hand to get anywhere…and although she knew that, as a god, his muscles would be in good condition, still, making an effort was alien to him so she guessed it would not be easy for him. Just as she had thought she should offer her help, she saw James offer his arm to Erie. No doubt about it. James was amazing. He'd adjusted to the events of the last day as if he'd been dealing with this all his life. Now he was offering a hand to a god and not even batting an eyelid.

"Careful, mortal. I don't need any more bruises you know."

"Cut it out, Erie. He didn't need to help you. You could show a bit of appreciation."

"It's okay, Corey, I can stand up for myself."

Eros stood back and leaned against the cave wall. "You two are funny."

"What do you mean?" said James.

"What are you talking about?" said Corey.

He shrugged. "Nothing."

Corey shuffled back and forth on her feet, forcing the blood back into her partially numb limbs. "You can't say something like that and not explain it, Erie."

"I can say whatever I want. I'm a god, remember."

"Don't get huffy with me — you didn't have to come here."

"That's right. I could have left you here all alone."

"Children. Please stop bickering!"

They stopped and turned.

Corey shuffled forward. "What do you want, Prometheus?"

"It seems I'm having a bit of trouble finding your sisters," he said.

She laughed. "As if I'm going to help you."

"Don't be too hasty, Corey," whispered James. "Get him to give you something in exchange."

She nodded slightly, hoping with all her heart that Prometheus hadn't heard.

"Soldiers — take the mortal."

Corey jumped toward him, almost tripping up on her tethered feet. "No! I'll tell you everything I know!"

Prometheus held up his hand, stopping the soldiers. "That is better. Tell me where Hera sent them."

She stood up straight and gestured to the ropes with her head. "First, how about you untie my hands and feet. I can't think straight when I'm confined."

He nodded to one of the soldiers. "Loosen her ties, but don't remove them."

She gave a dazzling smile to the soldier who was working on her wrists. "But, Prometheus, what can I do with all these big, strong soldiers around?" He winked at her as he finished and stood back. She looked down at the other soldier, who was busily untying the ropes from her ankles, and moved her feet apart, falling forward and tripping over him as she landed.

"What are you doing, woman?" bellowed Prometheus.

Corey struggled to right herself only to be hauled back upright by her captors. Prometheus' face was a thundercloud. He hated unpredictable behavior but bad luck. That's what she had planned for him. It drove him nuts and she hoped it worked.

"Tell me where your sisters are!"

She shrugged her shoulders. "I have no idea."

Prometheus charged forward and slapped her across the cheek "Don't play games with me, Terpsichore. You will not win. So tell me — where are your sisters?"

Her cheek was hot and it stung. She covered it with her hand to soothe it. "I'm telling the truth. We all disappeared at the same time. I have no idea where they are."

"Liar! How did Eros find you then?"

Oh crap. She didn't want him to turn on her friend now. "He found me by accident. Everyone knows he comes to Earth to play. It was a lucky coincidence is all."

He turned to Eros, who was trying his best to look nonchalant as he sat tied up on the cave floor. "Is this true, spawn of Aphrodite?"

Eros yawned. "I don't know if I should answer you after you insult my mother."

The soldiers turned and kicked him in the side.

Corey screamed. "Erie!"

He coughed, sat up straight and glared at her. "Don't worry about me, cuz. I'm fine."

"You won't be for long if you continue to defy me. Answer the question, you *kopros eater*!"

"All right. Jeez. Yes, it's true. I was scanning the area looking for a new love couple to play with and *bam* there's my Terpsichore dancing up a treat in downtown Sydney. No one was more surprised than I."

Prometheus shook his head. "I don't believe a word that comes out of either of your mouths." He started walking away from them. "Tie her up again, and make sure none of them can get out."

"Wait!" Corey called after him. "I fulfilled my end of the bargain. I told you what I know!"

He laughed. "Yes but you didn't tell me what I wanted to hear."

Ouch! The soldiers had made quick work of retying the ropes and one of them shoved her back to the ground. James just stared at her, confusion in his eyes. He opened his mouth to speak, but she held up her hands to stop him, while Erie just rolled his eyes.

When she was certain they'd understood, she turned her head toward the mouth of the cave and listened. After about fifteen minutes of silence she shuffled closer to James and turned her back on him.

"Quick. Grab the knife and cut me free," she whispered.

"Holy shit—where'd that come from?"

"I grabbed it when I faked falling over."

He laughed. "Good thinking Ninety-nine."

"Huh?"

"I think he's referring to an old TV show."

"Never mind," said James. "Let's just get out of here."

"Can't disagree there," said Erie as he shuffled closer to the others.

James took the knife from her trembling hands and started hacking. It took him a few tries to get it in the right direction to start cutting. "I'm sorry if I hurt you," he said.

"Just do it. I can cope."

"Not something I'm used to hearing from you, sweetie."

She grimaced. No, it wasn't. *What a selfish self-centered prat I was.* "I guess my priorities have changed a bit lately."

"I hate to interrupt, but can you spread your hands out a bit more, Corey, so I don't cut you?"

She did as he asked, her hands straining against the rough rope as he scissored the knife back and forth. Finally she felt it give and fall away and she pulled her hands free.

She turned and took the knife from James to untie her feet. She gave him a quick kiss on the lips before starting on the ropes at his wrists. As she worked, she heard a sound.

Someone was coming back.

She gave the knife back to James, who slid it under his sleeve as she returned to her place and wrapped the rope around her feet and hands, hoping like hell they wouldn't notice she wasn't tied up anymore.

She held her breath as the footsteps got closer. The soldier who had winked at her earlier came in and headed for James, indicating that he should stand.

In an instant she was on her feet and tripping him over with her outstretched foot, before grabbing his arms behind him. As he struggled she stood on his back placing her whole weight on the back of his neck to keep him from moving. She'd seen soldiers in her father's army do this in the training yard, and oh my goddess, it worked!

But her victory was short-lived as another soldier entered the cave and headed straight for her. Just when she thought their escape was doomed, James jumped up with a speed she would never have guessed he had and he tackled the second soldier to the ground. He must have given Erie the knife too, because he also appeared at her side with rope and started tying the soldier up. In minutes both were tied and gagged and sitting in the exact spots their prisoners had been.

James checked outside the opening and gave the thumbs up and they all ran out of there like bats out of hell.

Sometime later they stopped running, taking shelter behind a large rock. Corey had never felt so tired and exhilarated at the same time.

"Well, that was fun," said Eros.

James narrowed his eyes at him. "Speak for yourself. I'd rather be back home drinking a nice red."

Corey sighed. "I wish you were doing that too. I'm so sorry you got dragged into the fight between Prometheus and my father."

His face softened as he turned to her. His finger was soft as he stroked her cheek. "I'm not sorry. I want to help you."

"But you must hate me for putting you in danger."

He placed a finger over her lips. "Shh… Of course I don't hate you. I couldn't leave you here with that monster."

She turned her head to the side. *He doesn't hate me, but what does he feel for me? What would he think if he knew I loved him?* She shook her head. It wasn't the time for this type of thinking. They had to get out of there first.

"We're all here now, and the best thing we can do is find the way out," she said as she moved away from his distracting touch. "Erie, do you have any idea where we are?"

Eros shook his head, his face a mask. She gave him a second look, as she'd never seen him look so melancholy.

"Are you okay, Erie?" He looked up and gave her a thin smile. "Sure, toots. I was just thinking about Psyche. I'll be fine."

"You being away from her, that's all my fault too."

Eros reached for her and pulled her into a tight hug. "No it isn't. This is Zeus' fight, not yours. You're stuck in the middle and I don't blame you for any of it."

She smiled up at him. "You've always been my best friend, Erie. I hope Psyche appreciates you."

His eyes lit up at the mention of his beloved wife. "It's more a case of me thanking the gods every day for having her in my life."

She grasped Eros' hands then took a few steps backward. "I still can't believe you actually settled down."

"Neither can I, but then I never thought you would either."

She let go of his hands and stepped back even farther so she could see if James was listening to them. "I haven't settled down!"

James looked up. *Damn.*

She dropped her voice a few decibels. "I haven't settled down and I can't see it happening."

"Then why are you whispering?" said Eros, too loudly for comfort.

"I'm not..." she started. "I'm not whispering," she said in as normal a voice as she could muster.

James was openly staring at them both now, and Eros had a big goofy grin on his face. *Oh great.*

"Look, help me out here, Eros. Enough with the teasing."

He looked from her to James and back and nodded. "Okay, I get it. Just this once, and only because you're blushing."

She didn't think she was, but she touched her cheek to check. "I am not!"

"Gotcha!" he said as he rambled over toward the pathway on the other side of the rock.

Lucky for her he didn't see that she actually *was* blushing now.

They decided to head down the path and hope something looked familiar to Eros or Corey. It was a couple of hours since they'd come across anyone, and they'd ducked behind a clump of trees to avoid any interaction. Up ahead he saw a tall structure. It reminded him of the ruins of a Greek temple, which was probably right, considering where they were.

He stopped a few paces ahead of the others and pointed. "What's that place?"

Eros caught up with him. "The Palace of Hades."

He shuddered. "That place with the huge dog with three heads?"

"Cerberus. Yes, that's the place."

"Weren't we here before?"

Eros stared up at the structure, his intelligent eyes scanning from side to side. The loud roar of some unknown beast sounded through the air. "Yes, but we were on the other side. This is good news. Now I know where we are."

"I'm glad someone does because there's a few strange-looking flying creatures heading our way!"

Corey caught up with them and grabbed James by the shoulder. "Quick! Harpies! We need to hide!"

He didn't need to be told twice—those creatures looked like flying goblins on crack!

Their screeching made his blood run cold. The group turned and ran until James steered them into a forest of dense trees.

"We should be able to lose them in here," he said as they continued to walk into the middle of the scrub, which was getting thicker the farther they went.

Corey stopped and leaned over, panting to catch her breath. "We should stop here. They're probably looking around the perimeter to catch us when we leave."

Eros nodded. "This is true."

"Do these harpies have any weaknesses? Like—sleep?"

"They like stealing food," said Eros.

"We could distract them with food then. If we had any," said James.

Corey stood. "They do sleep. Eventually. After the parties finish."

"Well, by all means then, let's throw them a party."

"No need for sarcasm, Eros. I was just explaining to James."

James stepped in between them. "Hey, people, we need to pull together, not fight."

Corey sighed. "You're right, James. We need a plan to get us to the portal. Does anyone have any ideas?"

James scanned the scrub around them. "I'm not an expert on this place, or the creatures who live here, but if we use basic jungle combat rules, we should lay low until we're sure the harpies have moved on, and then get the heck out of here and find the track that leads to the portal."

Eros sat down under a bush and patted the dirt next to him. "You speak a lot of sense, for a mortal."

He laughed as he sat down and leaned against a tree trunk. "I'm sure you mean that as a compliment. I'm choosing to take it that way."

Corey's face lit up as she smiled at him then switched to Eros. "I'm glad to see you getting on so well, boys. How about we settle in and wait for the harpies to get bored and move on?"

"Good idea," he said and narrowed his eyes at Eros.

"Oh all right," said the God of Love. "I can take a hint and shut up."

* * * *

It took some time, but finally the sound of the harpies flying overhead subsided. Still, they waited an extra hour just to make sure that it was safe to move. The gods were definitely smiling down on them as a short time later they'd found the pathway to the portal.

Eros took the lead again with James in the rear. He wanted to make sure Corey was as close to the opening as possible she he could take her through quickly if Prometheus and his soldiers returned.

Finally it came into view and they moved toward the cave opening. James ushered Corey to enter but Eros stopped him.

"You have to go first. You are the mortal," whispered Eros.

"You told me Heracles did it. Why can't you?"

"He's half mortal. Heracles has the gift of strength but no powers. It has to be you."

James' heart stopped when he heard the sound of horses arriving behind them.

"Stop!" Prometheus called out.

James turned to find Prometheus signaling to his guards.

"Seize them."

Eros moved in front of James and Corey, throwing rocks to distract the soldiers.

"Move! This is your chance to be free."

Corey stood her ground. "Not without you. We all go together. Once we leave our powers will return, and Zeus and his soldiers will be waiting outside."

James dragged Corey by the hand, pulling her toward the portal. Eros backed toward them, his fists up and ready for action.

Prometheus roared. "Stop them!"

One of his soldiers shook his head and walked away from the group. "You heard her. Zeus is on the outside. I will not risk his anger."

Corey had known that she liked that soldier best when he'd winked at her back in the cave. It looked like being nice had won for her once again. *Who knew?*

"Fools!" Prometheus charged toward the group, but not fast enough to prevent them from passing through the portal.

A burst of light covered the entrance as they clambered up the stairs. Corey looked back as Prometheus' angry shouts cut off.

They were finally free.

* * * *

The palace displayed an opulence that far exceeded what James had thought it would be—if he'd ever believed it actually existed—which he hadn't until now.

Great expanses of marble covered the massive floor and white, gauze-like curtains hung from pillars that reached to the sky above—which, incidentally, he could see through a transparent dome he assumed to be the ceiling. It was so high, he couldn't really tell.

He lay on a bed as soft as clouds and was surrounded by platters of exotic fruits and pastries that were the most mouth-watering he'd ever tasted, and the water he sipped was the purest.

After soaking in a sunken bath, he'd slept for several hours. Now he lazed around, feeling unnecessary and unsure while he waited to see what happened next. Placing his arms behind his head, he took a long breath in, then blew it out slowly. This is the life Corey had grown up with. How the hell could he compete? *Fuck, did he want to try when he was bound to fail?*

Hell yes. When he thought he would never see her again, his gut twisted. There was something special between them, and even though they'd only been together for a few days, he knew he wanted her in his life. The problem was that he could never fit in here. Somehow, he'd have to convince her to come back with him, but would she? It might take time, but he knew his family would eventually accept her when they realized how he felt about her. If he was honest, he'd never wanted to be a Queen's Counsel anyway. That was his father's dream. The pressure to follow in his father's footsteps had been there all his life, although his father had always said it was his choice and no one elses. He'd never believed him then, even though he wanted to now. Not when he'd seen how delighted his father had been when he'd started his law degree. Still, he had chosen his own path, even if it hadn't entirely been his preference, but now he had a chance to change course. This time, it would be for himself, and not because of what had been pre-planned for him.

There was only one problem. How the hell did he convince a goddess, one of the Muses no less, to come live with him, for better or worse, in modern-day Sydney? He knew she felt something for him but he wasn't sure how much.

The question was academic anyway. Her father wasn't likely to allow her to go back to Sydney with him. He'd seen how relieved Zeus had been to get her back. Seen how much they loved each other, too. He had an uphill battle ahead of him, but he'd never been one to give up on a good fight and he wasn't about to now.

He sighed. *Where was Corey?* He hadn't seen her since they'd arrived and he missed her.

"You want her, don't you?"

Shit. He bolted upright. "Eros, you scared the crap out of me."

The blond giant walked over to a window seat and sat down, crossing his long legs at the ankles. "I am sure you will survive it. What I want to know is how you feel about Corey."

He wasn't used to sharing his feelings with a man, or with anyone for that matter. "What's it to you?"

"I repeat—you want her, don't you, James?"

He paused, aware that what he said now could affect his chances forever.

"I know that if I don't have her in my life, I'll miss one of the best things that ever happened to me."

Eros grinned. "Good answer. All right, now all we have to do is convince Zeus you are equally as good for her as she is for you." He stood up and turned to leave the room.

"Wait. I need help with that. How do I do it?"

Eros turned his head and looked over his shoulder, smiling. "Do not worry, James. I am not the God of Love for nothing. Love will prevail."

Chapter Five

"Are you sure Prometheus cannot escape again?"

"Do not worry, Terpsichore. My soldiers have captured him and placed him under the control of Hades. He cannot escape again."

"Thank you, Father. I fear for my sisters."

"Do not worry, my dear. With Prometheus out of the way we will find them. Now, tell me of this mortal you have befriended, my daughter."

Corey sat at her father's feet, sipping wine as she told her father of her time in Sydney as a dancer. "James? He is a wonderful man, Father. Leave him alone."

Zeus chuckled. "Why would I do anything to him, my dear Terpsichore? He saved your life. I owe him a great debt."

She slapped his foot playfully. "Since when has that ever stopped you from tormenting my lovers?"

"My dear, you do me a great injustice. I never interfere with my children's love life."

She snorted as she burst out laughing. "What about Demetrius? I remember you sent him to Sparta soon after we met. He definitely didn't volunteer. He worshiped the ground I walked on. "

"That was different. He was a weakling and an idiot. Entirely not worthy of you."

"What about Timothy?"

Zeus popped a grape into his mouth and swallowed before continuing. "I needed his expertise in Crete. You distracted him from his work. Olympus always comes first. You knew that at the time."

"Yes, I knew it, but I was a different person then. I wasn't really that attached to them… They were playthings to me as I was then. I've changed, and James is different. I love him."

Reaching for his goblet, her father smiled at her, his ageless face beaming with good humor. "Until you tire of him, I would think. How long do you think that will take this time? A week? A month?"

Corey stood up and walked to the window, staring wistfully out at the peaceful garden outside. "If I am lucky enough to be with James, I believe it will be an eternity."

"Ha. Lucky enough? He should bow down before your beauty and pay homage to your greatness and powers."

She turned to face him, speaking calmly, although her heart pounded. "No, Father. He is a good man, and I feel he is my destiny. Unfortunately, I have no idea how he feels about me."

"He will go with you because I command it."

She didn't want him that way. "No. Absolutely not. I want him to want me of his own free will. Don't you dare do anything, Father."

"I can always get Eros—"

Corey moved at lightning speed to be toe to toe with her father and spoke through clenched teeth. "No. No. No."

Zeus backtracked. "As you wish, my daughter. You have changed. You would not have cared this much in the past."

"I was a selfish, self-centered bitch. I am ashamed of how I was."

"You are entitled to get your own way. You are a goddess."

"But what is the point of having power and fame if you use them for the wrong reasons?"

Zeus smiled. "I think I like this James more and more."

"It was not only James who changed my way of thinking—it was also living among mortals, and learning to fend for myself. I like looking after myself—I could never go back to the old ways."

"So, what you are saying is that you wish to return to this Sydney place?"

"Yes, I am, Father. But only if James wants me there. I couldn't bear it if he moved on with his life without me. Please, Father, may I have your permission to return to Olympus if I wish?"

"You always had that, my daughter."

"But I was stuck there."

Zeus opened his arms and hugged Corey to his chest. "You only have to ask and I will return you. The power is within your heart. All I ask is that you spend some time here with your mother and me first."

"Of course, Father. I long to see my mother again. Does that mean I could have returned at any time? Eros was right?"

"You have to really want it, and I have a feeling you wanted to stay there for a time. In future, you will be aware of your feelings and will come for visits."

She threw her arms around him and hugged tightly. "Thank you, Father. You don't know how much your support means to me."

Zeus patted his daughter's back. "Oh, I think I do, my dear. I love your mother, remember?"

* * * *

James' gut was in knots as the servant showed him into a large chamber. He thought the room he'd been using was luxurious, but this room was a few levels higher than palatial. The transparent walls and ceiling gave the impression that they floated above the universe, which, considering who he was meeting, wasn't such a stretch. He hoped Corey would be there because he was scared stiff. It wasn't every day a guy got to meet the father of a girl he'd slept with, let alone cared about. It was something else to discover that her father was the *King of the Ancient Universe*. Just one look at her mischievous grin and he would relax. He rubbed his sweaty palms against his jeans and took an extra-deep breath. What he wouldn't give to be anywhere else right now. He stopped walking at the raised platform where the majestic figure sat on a large throne. Zeus was certainly an imposing figure. He was tall with mountainous shoulders, his hair the flowing white of the myths. If not for the lines on his face, he could easily be mistaken for a man in his forties — a very formidable man indeed.

His booming voice filled the large space like a megaphone. "Come." He must have been pretty scary to watch when Corey was growing up.

What the heck do you do when you meet a god? Bow? Get down on your knees? Who the hell knew?

"Do not worry, mortal. I do not expect you to bow down before me. This is not your world." He gestured for James to sit in one of the smaller seats next to the throne.

James lowered himself into the plush, cushioned seat. *He doesn't sound so scary.* "Thank you...sir. I am honored to meet you." Going for broke, he held out his hand to Zeus. "You are very famous in my world."

Ignoring the outstretched hand, Zeus roared with laughter. "I believe I am also a myth. As you can see, I am very much alive and definitely not a figment of anyone's imagination."

He smiled back. "I am having a hard time taking it in, but it's getting easier every minute I spend in this magnificent place."

Zeus moved forward, staring intently, his voice hushed. "You like it here? Do you wish to stay here?"

"Much as I think this place is so beautiful, I would not know how to fit in here. For starters, I have no powers."

"I can fix that with a wave of the hand."

"No. I mean—no thanks. That's not the life that I know. I need my own time and place."

Zeus frowned at him. "You are sure of that?"

He nodded. "I appreciate the gesture, but I can't see myself living here. I must work to support myself and I enjoy helping people. It's who I am. I couldn't cope with all this luxury if I had it all the time."

Zeus stood up, all seven feet of power and intimidation. "What? You think us soft and selfish?"

Oh hell. That didn't come out well. "No—not at all. What I meant is that I haven't had the necessary training to deal with the responsibilities that come with having power and position in a house as prestigious as this."

Zeus sat back down again, visibly relaxing. "Spoken like a true lawyer. I am impressed. My daughter was not lying when she said you are a good man."

She said that? Maybe there was some hope after all. He looked behind the throne to see if she was hiding behind her father. He wouldn't put it past her. "I was hoping to see Corey here this evening. I want to see for myself that she's okay."

"Terpsichore has left us."

"She's gone?" No! She left without saying goodbye. He stumbled as the pain hit him in the solar plexus.

"She has duties here. She has been summoned by her mother."

Another reason why it would never work. There was no point in hanging around. "In that case could I possibly impose on you to return me to my home?"

"You do not wish to stay and visit a while longer?"

Not now that Corey has moved on. "Thank you, but no. I too have duties and I have neglected them for too long."

"As you wish."

Zeus waved his hand and James found himself falling backwards, out of control. He thrust his hands behind him, hoping to break his fall...wherever he was falling to. Whirling colors surrounded him, hurting his eyes, so he closed them and waited. Within seconds he landed on some soft grass. Standing up, he opened one eye at a time, wary of what he might find.

He was in the park across the road from his apartment. He was home. *Thank God.* Although he should be happy, instead he felt numb. Hopefully, in a day or two, he'd get over it. A few days' hard work should do it.

Who am I kidding?

Reaching his door, he shoved his hand in his pocket for his keys. They weren't there. Remembering he'd left a spare set with the building supervisor, he turned for the stairs, stopping when he noticed a light under the door. What the—?

He pushed against the panels, opening the door. He hesitated at the threshold when the scent of vanilla filled his nostrils. Dozens of candles lit the room. An ice bucket, fully equipped with champagne, stood to the side of the couch. The orange label said 'Verve Cliquot', his favorite.

Corey. How did she know that?

Moving farther into the room, he looked around, puzzled. She had to be here somewhere. "Corey?"

A voice sounded from the bathroom. "James?"

She entered the room and he nearly swallowed his tongue. Her gorgeous body was draped in luminous, transparent gauze, leaving very little to the imagination.

"Corey…" he croaked. *Smooth, real smooth.* She smiled that wonderful smile at him. Her eyes sparkled and her skin glowed.

She was beautiful.

"I was trying to surprise you. I didn't expect you so soon."

"Oh, woman, I think I got here at just the right time."

Her face lit up even more, it that were possible. "You don't mind me being here then?"

He crossed the room and pulled her into his arms, kissing her forehead. "Are you kidding? I thought I'd never see you again."

"So would you have missed me if I hadn't returned?"

He tugged her closer against his body, showing her just how much he wanted her. "Does this answer your question?"

She rubbed against him, looking up into his face with a wicked smile. "I missed you too, James." She flicked her tongue over her lips and he couldn't wait any longer.

Their mouths met halfway in a meeting of souls that set off fireworks all around the room. He tasted her, drank in her essence and breathed her air. No one had ever made him feel like this — no one else ever would. The kiss went on for an eternity, but finished too soon.

"What — ?"

Lifting his head, he stared into her passion-filled eyes. "Don't be in too much of a hurry, my love."

There was plenty of time and he intended to enjoy her for a long while yet. From her uninhibited response, she enjoyed the journey as much as he. Continuing the trail down her body, he devoured her skin. Corey grasped his shirt, tugging it out of his jeans, ripping the buttons as she smoothed her hands over his chest.

"I want you naked. Now."

He grinned as he threw his shirt off his shoulders and unzipped his jeans.

She placed a finger over his lips. "Shh..." Taking his hand in hers, Corey led him to the bed and dragged him down beside her. She placed her hands either side of his face and pulled him close. Kissing her was like heaven but it was time for him to take some control here. He slid his hand under the material over her breasts and tugged. The whole concoction slid away, baring the alabaster skin of her breasts to his touch. He skimmed the tip of her nipples with his hands and she moaned into his mouth. The rosy nubs became more erect under his attention as he circled them and teased them into life. Breaking away from her mouth he started a trail of wet, open-mouthed kisses from the corner of her mouth and downward, inch by inch, savoring the exotic taste of her skin as he made his way to her breasts.

The quiet sighing sounds coming from her slightly parted lips intoxicated his senses as he covered one nipple with his mouth and suckled. She arched into him and covered his other hand, encouraging him to squeeze harder on her nipple. His teeth nipped and bit lightly on the tip. She moaned. He used his free hand to slip the rest of the material away from her body. Using his index finger, he traced a light line from her breast across her belly and to the edge of her silky curls. Swirling his tongue around her nipple he ran his finger over her labia. Oh God, she was so wet already. He had to feel this, so he slipped his middle finger inside. Her warm heat welcomed him, sucking him in further as his thumb rubbed her clitoris.

"Oh, James. Don't stop!"

Lifting his head he stared into her passion-filled eyes. "Not anytime soon, my love."

"I want you inside me now, James. I can't wait."

His jeans landed on the floor and he returned to the bed, lying between her thighs. He almost came there and then. "I can't wait either, Corey."

"Then don't."

He surged forward and entered her in one sliding movement. She met him lunge for lunge, surge for surge, until their heartbeats and breathing were one, and they collapsed together in exhaustion.

* * * *

Corey awoke spooned against a warm body with strong arms around her middle. She smiled as she remembered the night before. After hours of amazing, wonderful, mind-blowing sex yet again, it seemed that James did want her, but for how long she wasn't sure. It didn't matter as long as she had a chance to work on him. Twisting in his arms, she turned to face him and found his beautiful eyes smiling back at her.

"You're awake."

He kissed her eyelids one by one, before brushing his lips over her mouth. "I've been enjoying holding you while I waited for you to wake up. I was giving you another minute before the fun started."

She laughed. "You wish. Anyway, I have a few things to say and they can't wait."

He screwed up his face in a mock frown. "Such seriousness. We can't have that... Out with it. What did you want to say?"

"I'm here for good, James."

"I don't understand. I thought you would live on Olympus from now on."

"Do you want me to?"

"Hell no. Call me selfish, but I want you here."

Utter joy filled her heart, but she dared not believe what she was hearing. James sat up and drew her back into his arms, and she rested her head on his shoulder. "I was going to ask you to come back with me from Olympus, but your father said you'd already gone away. That you had duties."

"Oh he did, did he? That sneak. He knew I'd come back here. He sent me."

"Then why did he lie to me?"

She smiled. "My guess is he was testing your feelings for me. What was your reaction?"

"I asked him to send me back here immediately."

"Exactly."

Hang on. Something he'd just said came back to her. "What was that about asking me to come back with you?"

Cupping her face with each palm, he kissed her gently on the lips. "I care about you, Corey. When I found out you'd been kidnapped, I couldn't stand the thought of not having you in my life. I don't understand how I could have fallen for you after such a short time, but I'm not about to question it. So yes, Corey, I want you to stay. I can't make any promises that life will be rosy, I just know I want to live my life here with you."

Tears trickled down her cheeks and James wiped them away with his thumbs. "Don't cry. I didn't mean to upset you."

"You... You didn't," she blubbered. "I'm just so...happy."

"So what is your answer then? Do you want to stay with me and explore what we have together, or did I get it terribly wrong?"

"I want to stay with you. Why else do you think I was here last night when you returned?"

"Phew. I was worried there for a minute. I promise I'll get used to your powers, and I'll even visit your family if it means you'll stay here with me."

"There is no other place I want to be. You are my destiny, James, but I had to let you figure that one out by yourself."

"Do you goddess types always work so fast?"

"Only when we meet uptight lawyers who need to lighten up."

Smiling, he kissed her mouth once more. "That's never going to be a problem again. You've turned me into a wild man."

"Oh really? Just how wild are you?"

He rolled her onto her back, landing on top as she laughed in his ear.

"I'm very wild," he said as he grinned at her. "Let me show you just how much."

CALLING
CALLIOPE

Dedication

To Donna, Qwillia and Madeline for reading this story and offering suggestions, and a special shout out to Dawn and the Word Slinger Wrimo group. Without that awesome group and our word sprints, I would never have finished.

Chapter One

One more family settled in to a new life. Callie smiled when she closed the car door and strapped on her seat belt. They were her family — these abused and battered women and their children. Brave families who were courageous enough to start again. She loved each and every one of them. Even the hard cases who couldn't quite grasp the concept that perfect strangers were helping them and not expecting something in return. Eventually they came around, once they felt the love and acceptance. Just like she had.

Callie had a particular soft spot for the children. Kids were so resilient and they adjusted to the changes a lot faster than their mothers. Being in a safe place would do that.

She watched as Mardi, her best friend, and the manager of the women's shelter where she lived, climbed into the driver's seat and turned the key in the ignition. In looks they were as different as night and day, Callie with her brown eyes and long dark curls, and Mardi with her baby blues and short blonde bob, but they both cared deeply for the battered women and children they helped.

"All good?" asked Mardi.

Callie grinned. "All safe and sound. Jenny and her daughter are both tucked up in bed in their new home."

"No one followed you?"

"No, we changed trains twice. We went from here to the southern suburbs before finally getting to their house in Ringwood. No one could have followed us all that way!"

"That might have been a bit over the top, but at least we can be sure they're safe. How did Amy like the playground across the road?"

"She loved it. Jenny promised to take her first thing in the morning."

"That's great. You did a fantastic job with that family, Callie. I'm so glad you're here with us."

Callie reached over and wrapped her arms around her friend, giving her a big hug. "I love being with you, and trust me, I get more out of it than they do." She drew back a little and frowned. "It's not like I have anywhere else to be."

Her friend hugged her back. "I have a feeling the universe sent you to us for a reason, Callie, and I'm so glad you're here." Mardi gave her a mock punch to the biceps. "You're a bit quirky, but we love you for it."

Callie snorted as she broke contact. "Oh, for goddess sake, I'm no different to anyone else."

"See—you just proved my point."

"What are you talking about?"

"You're always saying things like *oh my goddess*, or *Zeus help us*. I've never met anyone like you, and I'm sure I never will again."

Callie laughed. "I'd like to think I'm unique, but I'm sure I'm not the only one who talks that way."

"I suppose that's possible," said Mardi. "But I do worry that when your memory comes back we will lose you."

Callie sighed. "It hasn't shown any signs of returning for six months, so I'm not sure it will." She clasped her friend's hand. "But know this—even if I do remember, I promise you I'll always be here to help you and the families."

"You shouldn't make promises you might never keep."

"Mardi, look at me," she said, tightening her grip. "I always keep my promises. I might not know much about myself, but my heart tells me this is the truth."

Her friend didn't seem convinced. "Just know that if you have another life to go back to, we will be happy for you."

The mobile phone rang and Mardi loosened her hands to answer it quickly, her face mirroring Callie's concern.

"No problem, we have a spare room right now," said Mardi into the phone. "Where are you? I'll come and get you." She grabbed a pen and paper from the dashboard and started writing. "Uh-huh...yep. Got it, see you in about fifteen minutes," she said, ripping the paper off the pad then tossed it to Callie. "And don't worry, honey, you'll be safe with us."

Mardi threw the gear stick into reverse before backing out of the driveway.

Callie keyed the address into the GPS. "Just the one?"

"No, two. She has a son. I'm not sure how old, but we'll work it out when we get there."

"There's a booster seat in the back that Amy used."

"Hopefully it will be fine. If not, we might have to break the law again."

"That's never been a problem for you before."

Mardi shrugged. "This is true."

"Good thing your boyfriend's a policeman."

"Yep. It helps when we need to push the boundaries a little."

"In two hundred meters, turn right," said the singsong female voice of the GPS.

Mardi whistled along to it as she drove, a little nervous habit she had which amused Callie no end.

"What? Are you laughing at me?"

Callie tried but failed to stop herself from smiling. "I wouldn't dream of it."

"Just be thankful I'm not singing."

"Yes, thank the gods!"

"Huh! You'll keep."

Luckily the GPS kept reasonably silent for the rest of the trip, while the pair prepared themselves for what they would find when they got there.

The street was deserted, but that wasn't unexpected as the address was an old church in an industrial area. The stench of uncollected garbage was high in the air. Most of these women were terrified of their husbands or boyfriends finding them, so hiding in the shadows was the norm.

"In the church?"

"That would be my guess," said Mardi as she opened the car door.

"Okay" — Mardi gestured to the side entrance — "I'll go in and you can stand watch."

"No problem. Be careful."

She watched Mardi glance down the barren street before pressing her hand against the tall, wood door.

Rusted hinges squeaked as she opened the door and walked inside the dark building.

It took less than two minutes before she reappeared with a small child in her arms and a petite blonde-headed woman following slowly behind her. The child, who looked about four years old from his size. His mother, like many before her, kept her head down, moving her eyes from side to side, checking to see if they were followed by whatever terror she was fleeing. Callie opened her door then climbed out. She moved forward and placed her arm around the woman's shoulders, squeezing gently.

"We'll take you somewhere safe, sweetie, don't worry."

She lifted her face, her eyes bleak. "You don't know Adam. He won't give up until I either go back to him or he kills me."

"We won't let that happen," Callie said.

The boy's mother didn't appear convinced and shook her head. "I mean it. He's tried to kill me before."

"He's a bully and a coward and we'll make sure he never hurts you again."

Her shoulders slumped and she sighed. "How can you promise that?"

"I can't promise, but I give you my word we'll do everything in our power to stop him from ever hurting you again."

Tears trickled down her face as her face crumpled. "I hope so, because this is our last hope. I can't go back."

Callie opened the rear door of the car and grabbed her a few tissues from the box they always kept handy.

She stepped back and waited for her to wipe her tears before she ushered her into the back seat. Callie reached over to take her bag but the woman held it close to her chest.

"What are you doing?"

"I was just going to put your bag in the boot."

"It's okay, I'll keep it with me."

"No problem. There's room in the middle."

"What about Jack?"

"That's your little boy's name?"

She nodded.

"I'm going to fit the booster chair so he can sit next to you. Mardi is taking care of him until I do that. Is that all right?"

She peered out the window, watching her son smiling and waving at her then lay back against the seat. "Okay, but we better hurry. Adam will be arriving home any minute and figure out we've left."

"No problem." Callie closed her door and quickly opened the boot to retrieve the child seat. It only took a couple of minutes before Jack was as snug as a bug and safely secured and they were on the road again.

Callie shifted in her place to face them, making sure she spoke softly. "My name's Callie, and this crazy woman driver is Mardi. Pleased to meet you both."

Mardi snorted. "She only says that because she can't drive herself. And anyway, she gets car sick."

The woman gave her a shaky smile. "Thanks. My name is Sarah, and my son is Jack."

Callie pulled out a soft toy from her bag then handed it to the little boy. "Nice to meet you, Jack. I have a little teddy here who needs a new friend. Would you like to be his friend?"

The little boy's face beamed. He leaned forward and grabbed it tightly with both hands. "Teddy!"

"I guess that's a yes then."

Sarah wiped another tear away as she touched her hand to her son's cheek. "He loves his stuffed toys, but we had to leave them behind. This is wonderful — thank you."

"You're very welcome."

Mardi increased her speed slightly and changed lanes.

Callie adjusted her side mirror then straightened in her seat. "Everything okay?"

Mardi sucked in a breath. "I hope so, but I'm not taking any chances."

Sarah gasped. "It's Adam. He's found us."

"Let's not panic just yet. What kind of car does he drive?"

"A blue Mazda."

"Only the most common car on the road at the moment, so I'm not getting too excited yet," said Mardi.

"It's him," whispered Sarah, her face stricken. "I knew he would find us."

Callie turned back to her. "You said he would only now be getting home from work. That would make it unlikely that it's him wouldn't it?"

Sarah shivered. "It should, but he has this sixth sense. He always knows when I'm planning on leaving. All the other times he's come home before I've gotten out the door."

"What's his number plate?"

"He has a vanity plate. It says *The Boss*. He owns his own business, but he used to be a cop."

Callie muttered under her breath. "Fitting — obviously how he sees his role with you."

Mardi checked the mirror again. "I'm pretty sure that Mazda has a vanity plate but I can't read it."

"Let's see if he reacts when we move," she said, easing the car into another lane.

Callie kept an eye on the mirror. "He changed lanes as well. He's sitting two cars behind now."

"There's a traffic light up ahead. I'll see if I can catch it before he has a chance to draw closer."

The light turned red just before they approached but Mardi sped through. The blue car ducked out to the other side of the road before following them, almost colliding with a truck that was crossing the other way.

"It looks like we've got our man," said Callie, adjusting her seat upright to get a better view.

Mardi sighed. "Okay then, hang on, folks—make sure your seat belts are tight because we're in for a bumpy ride."

Mardi maneuvered the car across two lanes and hung a leftie, only to immediately swerve right into the driveway of a nursing home and around the back of the building. She stopped the car behind a shed and turned off the ignition.

"Shout out to the gods—that was amazing driving," said Callie once her breath had returned.

Mardi twisted around to check on the others. "I think we lost him. Everyone okay?"

Jack giggled in the back seat, his new teddy held tightly in his little chubby arms. "That was fun! Can we do that again?"

Sarah's face was pale as she sat gripping the seat so tight that her knuckles were white. "I don't think so, darling. Mummy doesn't like fast rides remember."

Jack reached over and touched his mother's arm. "That's okay, Mummy. I love you."

Sarah sobbed as she wrapped her arms around her son. "I love you too, sweetie. Soon we won't have to be scared anymore."

Mardi fired up the car, the engine purring as she reversed out from behind the shed. "That's right, kiddo. We're going to help you and your mummy find a nice new home."

Jack giggled. "Awesome!"

Sarah struggled to keep back a smile. "That's his new favorite word."

"Well I think it's a great word. An awesome word hey, Jack?"

"Awesome!"

The rest of the trip to Serenity was without incident, which was lucky because Callie's heart was pounding right up until they parked the van in the garage in the back lane.

After they'd walked inside, Mardi went into the kitchen to put the kettle on and Callie showed Sarah and Jack to their new room.

"The beds are made up, and there are towels in the cupboard. The bathroom is to the left," said Callie while she sat Jack down on the smaller bed.

"Thank you for all you're doing."

"We only want to help."

"Yes, but what Mardi did today was going above and beyond. I didn't want to put anyone else in danger."

Callie shrugged. "It goes with the territory. Since I've been here we've had to dodge quite a few angry husbands. If you weren't in that situation, you wouldn't be coming here for help."

"So why do you do it?"

Callie smiled. "Mardi found me when I needed help, so now I give back by helping others. The funny thing is that I love it. I never expected to, although I'm not sure why that is."

"So you ran from an abusive relationship too?"

"No, my problems were different, but we don't need to go into that now. Let's get you settled in. We're making tea in the kitchen if you're interested, but remember, if you want time to yourself, that's fine too. Dinner's usually at six."

Sarah nodded. "Jack's tired, so we might stay here and have a nap. We'll come down for dinner. I'm sure Jack will be hungry."

"I'm hungry now, Mummy."

Sarah brushed her son's hair across his forehead, moving it out of his eyes. "I have a banana for you in my bag. That will do until dinner."

"Okay."

"He's such a good boy, Sarah. You've done a wonderful job with him."

"Thanks, he's the joy of my life."

* * * *

Oeagus was a descendant of Atlas, the son of Charon, a river god and the King of Thrace, but he still could not find his wife. Six months had passed since Calliope and her sisters had vanished from Mount Olympus and still no word. He believed it was all Hera's doing, but he couldn't prove that. Zeus was being very tight-lipped about the whole incident, but why he showed any loyalty to that wretched woman he would never know.

He closed his eyes and remembered her beautiful smile and sparkling eyes. He should have insisted she stay with him on his throne instead of traipsing around with those flighty sisters of hers, but in his heart he knew she would never agree to that. She lived for the arts and she adored telling those amazing stories to the courts. She'd always loved to be in the center of the action so he understood her need to travel with her sisters. It had been part of the reason they had been separated when she'd disappeared. That and a certain, stupid argument. He wished she were here now so he could clear all that nonsense up, but she wasn't, and he was beginning to despair of ever finding her. Terpsichore had been found in a strange land and had returned a changed woman. He wasn't sure how that had happened, but he didn't want to find Calliope too different from the woman he'd fallen in love with. Sure, she was a goddess, and as a goddess she exhibited certain expected behaviors, but when they were alone she was just a woman, and he a man, and he wanted that back again.

He sighed. Wishing for it wasn't doing him any good. He was a man of action so he needed to do something himself. All the gold and all the spies in the land weren't working and it was time for him to step up.

As he walked to the window, he stared out at his kingdom below. From where he stood, the view of the majestic mountains to the north reminded him of his father, Atlas. What would he make of this mess? To the south the Aegean Sea sparkled, the clear blue waters rippling as the large boats traveled into the harbor. In the courtyard below smoke billowed from where his slaves worked, forging weapons from stone over the many fires that burned there. The smells of the molten iron mixed with the aroma of baking bread from the kitchens.

He scanned the area, spying his servant. "Leonidis. Come."

He paced the room while he waited for the tall servant to enter.

"How can I assist you, my King?"

"I need to speak to Eros. Send a messenger to collect him. Tell him it is of the utmost urgency."

The servant hid a smile. "That will be easy, my King. He has just arrived in the palace and seeks audience with you."

The tall blond god of love sauntered into the room. "What's this, Gus? You're psychic now? You've been spending time with my wife?"

Oeagus approached his friend and pulled him into a hug, slapping Eros on the back with his fist in the traditional greeting of warriors. "I'm pleased you are here, cousin. I need your help."

"If it concerns Calliope then I have some news."

"You've found her?"

"Yes, but…"

"No buts. We go and collect her at once."

Eros held his hand up. "It is not as simple as that."

"What do you mean? We go. We find her. We bring her back. What is there that is not simple?"

"Well for starters, she's in the same land where I found Terpsichore."

"Good. Corey can help us."

"She is not in the same city, which is why it took me longer to find her."

"So why is this a problem?"

"It wouldn't be, except for the other problem."

"Other problem? What problem is that? Is Calliope injured? Is she unwell? I will kill anyone who has touched her!"

"No, I believe she is quite well."

Oeagus smashed his fist against the wall. "Then what is the problem?"

Eros flinched. "She has no memory of her life before arriving there. She doesn't know who she is, or that she's a goddess."

"She will know me. I am her husband."

Eros picked up a grape from the table then popped it in his mouth. "That's the thing, my impatient friend. She doesn't remember anything."

Gus rushed to the door. "I must go to her. Bring her back here so we can cure her."

"I don't think that's going to work either. I tried to use my powers to return her memory when I found her, but it didn't work. There has to be another reason why she has forgotten her life."

Oeagus turned around. "What in Hades could that be?"

"I don't know, but I suggest we approach her with caution. I consulted the *Akeso* before I came here and she said it was beyond her powers to cure her. She insists we convince Calliope to come here of her own free will, and she may recover her memories in time. To force her in such a fragile state might make the memory loss permanent."

"But what if she won't agree to leave?"

Eros smiled. "You managed to charm her into marrying you once. You can do it again."

"But you say she won't remember me."

"Then you'll have to be on your best behavior." Eros laughed.

"This is not a laughing matter, Eros."

"I'm sorry, but I just can't see you being subtle."

"I can be subtle. I am a diplomat and a king."

"My point exactly. You speak and people listen. It won't work that way in the land of Australia, where your Calliope has been living for the past six months."

"Then you will teach me about this strange place."

Eros scratched his chin. "I suppose I could."

"Eros—I beg of you. Help me. I will defend you against Ares the next time he attacks if you will do this for me."

"When you put it that way, how can I resist?"

"I am in your debt. I will not forget this," he said. "Tell me what I need to do."

"First we need to do something about your clothing."

Oeagus glanced down at his toga and robes. "What is wrong with my attire?"

Eros threw his arm over Oeagus' shoulder and led him out of the room. "For starters, if you walk around like that, Calliope is bound to think you a madman and have you locked up."

"Good thing I have you to show me the way then." He smiled.

Eros chuckled. "Let me tell you about this strange clothing called jeans."

Chapter Two

Callie sat quietly and sipped her coffee. If there was one thing she'd fully embraced since losing her memory it was good coffee. The first time she'd tasted a cappuccino had been love at first mouthful. She wondered if she'd ever tried it, but she'd almost given up thinking about what had come before. Six months had gone by and the only remnant of her past was her apparent speech affectations and a total lack of knowledge of the world she now found herself in. Questions constantly plagued her. Where had she come from? What had she left behind? Thank the gods for Mardi. If she hadn't taken her in and gotten her medical attention, she'd probably be in a mental health facility right now. It also helped that Mardi's boyfriend, Chris, was a cop. He'd tried for a while to see if he could find her real identity, but she hadn't matched any missing persons' reports he'd scoured, so he'd given up for now, with a promise to keep an eye out for news.

Given her work at Serenity, she often wondered if she was also running from someone, or from a bad situation. Maybe it was something she didn't want to remember, for whatever reason. It did puzzle her that no one seemed to be searching for her, and if she were honest, it hurt just a little. Wasn't she important enough to someone that they wouldn't move mountains to find her?

She sighed before taking another sip of coffee. Maybe it was best if she concentrated on the here and now. She could control that, unlike the unknown past that eluded her. The outdoor café on the edge of a park was one of her favorite places. The smell of freshly ground coffee never failed to entice her in, and the large terracotta pots overflowing with annuals in bloom reminded her of someplace she couldn't quite put name to. She laughed, remembering the story she'd told Jack that morning. He'd been enthralled by her tale of ancient beings, gods and special powers. He'd particularly loved the monsters, but she'd had to make sure that they were vanquished before the end of the story so he wouldn't have nightmares. She had no idea where the stories came from. Perhaps she'd been an ancient history buff in her past life? At least she was putting it to good use. She enjoyed spending time with the children. They were the innocent victims in the battles between their parents, much as the women were victims of the monsters who were their ex partners. She was glad she could contribute to helping these families heal. In a small way it was helping her to heal too.

A shadow loomed in front of her, obscuring her sight of the pot of flowers she'd been admiring. Her raisin toast was placed in front of her and she looked up to thank the waitress. Instead, a large figure towered over her.

"Can I help you?" she asked.

The figure moved closer and she got a better view. Tall, blond and giant would have been three words to describe him. Compelling, gorgeous and hypnotic would have been three more. Her heart raced as she took in his presence.

He spoke to her. "Do you not recognize me?"

Her heart stopped and she held her breath. She struggled to answer him, "You know me?" She wasn't sure he would hear her since her voice was so raspy.

He flinched. "Yes, I know you," he growled.

She gazed around the room and noticed the other patrons were staring at them both. "You'd better either sit or leave. We're making a spectacle here."

He roughly pulled a chair out then sat directly across from her, taking her hand in his as he leaned forward on his elbows.

His larger-than-life presence was overwhelming, and the way he stared at her with his clear blue eyes taking in every inch of her face was unnerving, but grasping her hand — that was totally unacceptable.

She snatched her hand back and placed it under the table and on her lap. "Do not touch me without my permission." The skin tingled where he had touched her and her heart thumped so loud she could hear it in her head. "You may think you know me, but I have absolutely no idea who you are."

The giant recoiled and she almost regretted her abrupt words when she saw the raw pain in his face.

"I am sorry," he said. "I did not mean any offense. It has been six long months since we were last together."

Oh my goddess, maybe he does know me. She took a deep breath before letting it out slowly. "Who do you think I am?"

"You are my light, my love. Without you I have been but an empty shell."

She blinked. *Is he for real?* She couldn't remember hearing anyone speak in such a fashion since she'd been here. "You're poetry is nice, but you didn't answer the question. Who do you think I am?"

He smiled. "It was not poetry, my love. You are Calliope, the daughter of Zeus," he said, staring into her eyes intently, "and my wife."

Did he really say I'm his wife? Now she knew he was crazy. She tried to laugh, but it came out more like a squeak. "What have you been drinking?"

"I am not intoxicated, if that is what you mean. I speak the truth."

"You're insane," she said, pushing her chair back as she stood up. "I think I'd better leave."

He also got up, taking a step closer toward her. "My deepest apologies, Calliope. Eros warned me you would not be ready, but I could not wait. I am sorry. I have missed you so much and I did not mean to frighten you."

Her chest felt tight and her breathing quickened. She backed away and maneuvered toward the exit, her legs feeling like jelly. "It's okay. I think you have the wrong person, and quite frankly I think you need to see a doctor."

"I do not have the wrong person, but I will give you time to get used to this news. Fear not, my love," he said while drawing her hand to his lips. "I will protect you with my life, but I will not force myself upon you."

His hot breath tickled across her skin, sending shivers all over her body. She should not be so affected by this crazy stranger, but somehow she was. She reclaimed her hand and continued walking out of the café. "It was nice meeting you, but I think I'll go now."

He followed her onto the street. "I will accompany you to your home."

"No!" Alarm bells went off in her head. *Maybe he was sent by one of the husbands of the women at the shelter?* "I will see myself home. It's been fun, but I think it would be better if we say our goodbyes now."

The giant frowned. "Oeagus. That is my name, but you call me Gus in private. Perhaps you will dream of our life together?"

"I don't think so," she said.

His eyes lit up in amusement. "We will see. I will leave you now. I'll be back for you when you are ready to believe."

She hailed a passing cab and ran to the curb as it stopped.

She threw her bag into the back seat before climbing in. "Not going to happen."

When the cab drove off down the street her breathing markedly increased in rate.

The cab driver turned to her and asked, "Are you all right, lady?"

"I'm fine," she rasped. "Just take me to the address I gave you."

He didn't seem convinced of her health, but like most taxi drivers, he probably didn't want to get involved so he turned back to the road and drove off.

She fought to regain her equilibrium as the car wove in and out of Melbourne traffic. She wasn't sure what to make of the situation. The man was obviously mad. Either that, or Sarah's husband had hired him to help him find the refuge. Whatever the reason, she was going to steer clear of him. For all she knew he could be some obsessed stalker from her past. Someone with a delusional belief in a relationship with her. She'd read about those kinds of men when she'd researched the best way to help the women at Serenity. That had to be it because seriously — the daughter of Zeus? That would make her some sort of goddess. She covered her mouth to stifle her laugh. *How ridiculous!* The more disturbing notion was the idea that she was connected to that crazy, albeit gorgeous giant. She'd know if she was married, wouldn't she? And she certainly wouldn't be related to someone as delusional as him.

The taxi dropped her off at the terminus near St Kilda Beach. She jumped on a tram and headed the rest of the way home to the south-eastern suburb of Glen Huntly, where Serenity was situated. Mardi was in her office when she walked in the door. She flopped down into the visitors' chair and sighed.

Mardi raised her head from her keyboard, narrowing her eyes as she spied Callie. "What's up with you?"

"The weirdest thing happened to me just now."

"Yeah? So don't leave me hanging. Tell me!"

"I met a man who says he's my husband."

Mardi jumped to her feet. "You're kidding!"

"No, and it gets better. Apparently I'm a goddess."

Mardi giggled. "Well that explains the way you talk."

"Huh? You can't really believe this? I mean, it's absurd. There are no gods and goddesses. It's mythology."

"Of course it's absurd, but hey it couldn't hurt to do a search on this guy. Just for fun."

"I don't believe you said that, Mardi. You're meant to be the sensible one, and you're encouraging me to look up an imaginary character."

"I didn't say I believed him, but wouldn't it be fun to Google it? C'mon. What would it hurt?"

Callie laughed. "I can see what you're doing. You're trying to lighten the moment so I won't dwell on it."

"Darn. You figured out my evil plan. But seriously, aren't you even a little curious about this person he says you are? And what about him? Don't you want to know more?"

"Well…" She grinned, leaning forward to turn the computer screen sideways so they could both see it. "Okay, so maybe I am a little curious."

"Ha! I knew it," said Mardi as she opened a new browser. "What did you say your supposed name is?"

"Calliope."

"As in the name we already call you—one of the Muses?"

"I guess. It's the only one I know of."

"We called you Callie because the sheet thing you were found in had a symbol for Calliope embroidered on it. This is seriously weird. And you really do know a lot about this Greek mythology stuff." She shrugged, typed in the name then pressed 'enter' while they watched the search engine fill up with pages of links.

"I'll admit it's strange, but we all assumed I'd been to a costume party. I'm thinking that someone found out, and they're exploiting that fact now. Try searching for images."

Mardi added a few more key words and hit 'return'. A page full of images opened up, some of them statues, and some paintings. One stood out in the middle of the page.

"Oh my God, Callie—it could be you!"

Callie leaned in and stared at the screen before sitting back in her chair. "Don't be ridiculous. That picture is nothing like me."

"Callie…it could be your twin."

"You're imagining it," she said as she took control of the mouse. She clicked on the search engine and immediately typed in the name of Oeagus.

Several images appeared and all of them bore an uncanny resemblance to the blond giant who'd accosted her in the coffee shop. *How could this be?*

Mardi pointed at the screen. "Oh look. Here's one with his wife — Calliope!"

Callie gasped at the painting. The clothing and the hair were stylized, but the facial features of the couple could be that man — and herself. "Someone hired an actor who looks like him. That has to be the explanation."

"You have to admit, the resemblance between you and that woman is uncanny, and this guy could be the long lost twin of that actor in that movie *Thor* — wow! Are you sure he's not your husband? Heck, he's so cute, don't you want to pretend a little?"

"Mardi!"

She burst out laughing. "You know I was joking, right? But hey, if I was going to be 'pretend' married to anyone, someone like Thor would definitely be my choice."

Callie shook her finger at her. "I'm telling Chris."

Mardi placed her hand over her heart. "Some friend you are! All right, I'll stop with the teasing now. But wow — it's amazing how much you are like that Calliope person, and from your reaction, this guy — Oooaygus...or however his name is pronounced, is similar to the one from the coffee shop."

"Gus."

"Huh?"

"Gus. He told me I call him Gus."

"I can't believe I'm saying this, but does anything about him or what he said ring a bell? Seem familiar even a little bit?"

"No, nothing at all."

"Geez, you answered that quickly. Are you sure?"

Was she? Did that tingle across her skin where he'd touched her mean anything? *No.* "Yes, I'm sure. If I believed this wild story, you'd be calling up that doctor friend of yours again. You know — the one for crazy people?"

"I think you're one of the sanest people I know. If you believe any of this, you're sure to have a logical reason." Her eyes twinkled with amusement. "If you did," she said, closing the computer browser.

Callie narrowed her eyes at her and frowned.

"But of course you don't."

"Exactly."

* * * *

In her bed later that night, Callie tossed and turned for hours before finally falling asleep some time past midnight. Since she'd lost her memory, dreams had eluded her, but tonight that all changed.

The man who claimed to be her husband certainly haunted this dream, just as he'd predicted. It wasn't enough that he was in her head for most of her waking time, but now here he was in full living color, and apparently she wasn't just seeing him, but her body was reacting to the whole situation as well. He moved over her as she lay against silken sheets.

She gasped. "Why are you here?"

"To bring you pleasure," he said.

"So you say," she squeaked when he nuzzled her neck, sending tingles across her body.

"And to give you a memory." His voice rumbled against her ear.

She opened her mouth to protest, but he cut her off with his mouth, teasing her with his tongue as he delved inside.

It felt right. Familiar. Ecstasy.

She moaned.

"Though your mind forgets, your body remembers," he whispered. He cupped her face with his hands, stroking her cheek gently with his thumbs.

"I don't want to remember," she murmured. "It's too difficult and it makes my head hurt."

"Then don't think," he said. "Just feel."

She opened her eyes and stared into his. "I can't."

He smiled, the corner of his lips turning up into a grin. "But this is only a dream. You can do anything in a dream."

Her mind was telling her to stop right there, but her body, now that was a different story. Should she just go with it? It's just a dream. "Oh, what the heck."

She reached behind his head, drawing him back.

The first touch of his lips was explosive. They moaned in unison, tongues tangling and tasting, taking everything they could find, and more. He took hold of her arms, raising them above her head with one hand as he trailed open mouth kisses from her lips to her neck and below. She arched her back, wanting him to find her breasts. She thrust them forward in anticipation and he didn't disappoint, suckling the tips one at a time while he tweaked the other with his long fingers. She hitched her breath, the air coming in and out of her lungs rapidly to match the pulse she heard pounding inside her head. The slight edge of pain was an exquisite pleasure. She didn't want it to stop, but the pressure was building below and she needed him elsewhere.

"Please..."

He lifted his head. "What is it, my love?"

"I need you inside me," she whispered.

She could feel his smile against her skin. "I need you also, and you will have me," he said, as he twisted her nipples.

She drew in a deep breath and arched forward again and he began another assault on her body, trailing slow kisses around the curve of her breasts. "Please – I can't wait."

"I can't either, but I want to savor your body," he said. "Trust me, my sweet wife. It will be worth the wait."

"But this is my dream…"

"Exactly, my love. This is why I will make it an experience you will remember for long after you wake."

"Argh…" *she moaned.*

He smoothed his warm hands down over her hips and inside her thighs, moving her legs apart as his kisses reached her sex.

He slid his clever fingers inside her while his tongue found all of the places where the pleasure was at a blissful high. The pressure inside her womb grew more urgent.

She was desperate, opening and closing her hands and grasping at the sheets, not knowing what to do with them. "Please…"

He didn't listen. He continued his sensual assault until her body was wound up tighter than a ten-day clock, before he moved into place and slid inside her.

Home. This is what she'd been waiting for.

He took her hands in his and laced them together.

"My love," *he sighed.* "I've found you at long last."

They moved together, like two pieces of a puzzle, fitting as if they were meant to, riding each other until the moment of climax, when the intense release rushed through her body in wave after wave of sensation.

* * * *

She woke hours later, covered in sweat with someone tugging on her hand. *Huh?*

"Callie," said someone with a little voice.

She opened one eye. "Jack?"

"Wake up, Callie."

She rolled over onto her back then pushed herself upright. "Is everything okay?"

"I'm cold."

She glanced at the clock by her bed. It was almost five-thirty in the morning. "Is your mummy okay?"

"She's sleeping," he said.

"You want to jump in with me? It's nice and warm inside."

She lifted the blankets, and he nodded, climbing in and settling on her lap.

"You smell nice," he said as he sniffed the air. "My mummy smells nice too."

"Mummies always smell nice."

He turned his head, staring up at her, scrunching his little face. "Are you a mummy?"

Her heart stopped. How many times had she asked herself the same thing? *I would know if I had children, wouldn't I?* She took in a breath then let it out slowly, hoping she spoke the truth. "Not yet."

"My mummy's sad."

Jack snuggled. "I know, sweetie. We need to cheer her up. What does she like to do?"

He scratched his chin and closed his eyes. "She likes chocolate."

"Ah, the food of the gods. She has good taste. It just so happens that Mardi has been teaching me to cook, and the first thing I learnt was chocolate cake. Would you like to help me cook one for your mum?"

Jack clapped his hands together and let out a whoop. "Awesome!"

"Okay then, let's tiptoe downstairs so we don't wake anyone and we can surprise her with a gorgeous cake made especially for her by you."

"Yay!"

"Shhh...we don't want to wake the others."

"Sowwy," he whispered.

Oh, my goddess, this kid is so cute.

As they walked down the stairs together she wondered again if she had a child of her own. If Gus really was her husband, did they have a child together? She pressed a hand over her heart to ease the pain, vowing to ask Gus at the first opportunity.

In the kitchen Callie laid out the cookbook on the bench then sat Jack in a booster chair at the table. Once all the ingredients were out and she'd turned the oven on, she measured the dry ingredients before helping Jack to pour them in the large bowl. She left him stirring them with a wooden spoon while she cut up the butter. She added it to the sugar and blended it with the eggs. After they'd scraped the bowl and poured the batter into the cake pan, she let Jack lick the spoon.

"Good thing we haven't had a shower yet." She laughed as Jack slipped his tongue down his chin to catch the drips from the cake mix.

"You have chocolate all over your face, Callie. You're funny!"

She rubbed her hand over her cheek to wipe the batter off and started giggling. "So I have. Aren't we a couple of messy devils?"

Jack giggled back. "We're not devils. We're angels. We're making cake."

Callie filled the sink with soapy water and placed all the dirty dishes inside. "I suppose we are. But we won't be angels until we tidy up, so come with me to the bathroom, little man, and we'll fix that right away."

"Okay," he said as she helped him out of the chair. "Mummy likes me to wash my face and hands."

"We'd better make sure we do a good job then, huh?"

"Awesome!"

* * * *

Fifteen minutes later, Jack and Callie were shiny and clean and the kitchen was once again spotless. The kettle had just boiled when a frantic Sarah raced into the room.

"Jack! Where have you been? I woke up and you were gone."

"I'm sorry, Sarah, he came to my room and I thought you might need a sleep in."

Jack's top lip trembled. "We made cake, Mummy."

Sarah ran across the room to her son and hugged him hard. "I'm sorry, Jack. I'm not mad. I love it that you made cake."

"I wanted to make you happy, Mummy."

She wiped away a tear. "Thank you, Jack. I am happy you did that for me." She spied Callie and nodded. "And thanks for helping him."

"Don't thank me yet. The cake isn't finished and since it's only the second cake I've ever made, it might not taste all that great."

"You've never made cake before?"

"Not until last week, but it was an easy recipe."

"Don't believe her, it will be delicious if her first effort is anything to go by," said Mardi as she walked into the room. "It took me years of practice to get the cake to rise just a little, and Miss Perfect here throws it all together and it's as good as Adriano Zumbo's best."

"I wouldn't go that far..."

"Well it was yummy, and that cake baking in the oven smells divine too."

The timer went off and Jack jumped up and down as he danced around the room. "The cake is cooked. The cake is cooked."

Sarah caught him by the hand. "Slow down, Jack, loud noises can make the cake fall."

Callie lifted the cake out of the oven before she placed the tin on the stovetop "Don't worry, it's fine. We'll leave it until it's cool before we get it out of the tin."

"See what I mean?" said Mardi. "She even talks like a pro."

Callie poked her tongue at her friend and pulled three mugs out of the cupboard. "Who's for a cup of tea?"

"I want cake," said Jack.

Callie ruffled his hair and kissed him on the forehead. "We'll have it for morning tea, sweetie. It's only breakfast time now."

"But we made it, Callie."

Her heart melted. He was such a gorgeous boy. "I know, sweetie, and we'll have it soon, but it has to cool down, and then we need to ice it. How about we have some cereal while we wait for it?"

Sarah smiled at her gratefully. "Cornflakes are your favorite, aren't they, Jack?"

"I love cornflakes!"

"What a coincidence," said Callie. "So do I."

* * * *

Gus paced back and forth in this place called a hotel. The small room contained only one bed, a small table and chair, and a very small bath. The owner must have had a proclivity for a strange green color that covered the walls and the bed coverings. It reminded him of the olives that grew on his land, and he shuddered to think what his wife would think of such primitive surroundings. Seeing Calliope yesterday had been wonderful, but he hadn't realized how difficult it would be having her not remember him at all. Not even a flicker of recognition had crossed her face. *How could that be?* His brain knew that it might take time, but his heart had been hoping that one glimpse at her beloved husband would be enough for all her memories to return. Whatever had caused them to go must be stronger than he'd thought. Even his visit to her dreams had not helped. He had to take things slower. He might have made his chances worse by blurting out who she was. She had seemed to think he was mad. What had this world done to her? Did they have no goddesses and deities in this place?

He really should have asked Eros more questions.

A knock on the door interrupted his thoughts.

"Come," he called out.

He stood for a minute, but nothing happened, so he walked over and opened it. A servant with a tray of food stood outside.

"Don't just stand there, bring it in," he said.

"You better give him a coin," said Eros, who had a knack of appearing out of thin air when food was served.

"Why? He is a servant."

"Don't let him hear you say that," whispered Eros. "Give him a coin. It's a custom. They call it a tip."

Gus pulled out the leather purse from his pocket. He tipped a couple of coins into his hand then tossed a couple at the room service waiter. "For your trouble."

The waiter glared at the small gold coin and frowned. "What's this?"

"It's a gold coin, what do you think it is?"

"Is it real?"

Eros scoffed. "Of course it's real. Now leave before I take it back."

The waiter smiled and backed out of the room quickly. "Thank you, sir."

"You're welcome," said Eros. He closed the door and turned back to Gus. "Really, Oeagus, you need to learn some modern manners."

"What do you mean?"

"There are no slaves here. These people are paid to work."

"Then why, pray tell, was I required to give him a 'tip'?"

"Because people who carry bags and push trays are paid little, and these tips supplement the pittance they make."

"Doesn't seem very efficient to me. Why don't they just buy slaves and be done with it."

"Because slavery is outlawed here in this time."

"Why?"

"Because people in this time are free. As much as they can be anyway."

"My slaves are not prisoners. I provide food and shelter and they are treated fairly. They want for nothing and they work for me willingly."

"Not everyone treats their slaves well like you do, Gus. Just remember what I said, there are no slaves here."

"Fine. No slaves. What else have you forgotten to tell me?"

Eros laughed. "There are still many things about this land that puzzle and intrigue me."

"You are no help then."

"I take it you have yet to succeed with Calliope?"

Oeagus sighed. "No. She thinks I'm a lunatic."

"You didn't tell her who you are, did you?"

"I couldn't help myself."

Eros grabbed a handful of grapes from the tray and made himself comfortable on the couch. "I told you to take it slowly. Spend time with her—charm her if you have to."

"Once I saw her I wanted her to remember me immediately. I thought it might trigger something, but I was wrong."

"Hmm. That's going to make it a little harder. Do you have another plan?"

"I thought I would try and make friends with her. Maybe offer to help at that place where she is living."

Eros rubbed his chin. "I'd be very careful about going to that house. For some reason she seems to go to great lengths to keep its location a secret. When I first found her she changed her mode of transport three times before heading home. It took all of my powers just to keep up with her."

Oeagus cursed. "Why would she keep it a secret? Is she in danger?"

"I don't know," said Eros, scratching his head. "Maybe. It seems that the women who go there are running away from their husbands. A disgruntled husband might not like that."

"Why would my Calliope be helping women to escape their husbands?" asked Oeagus. "Was she not happy with me?"

"I don't know, Oeagus. You will have to peer into your heart and answer that question yourself.

Oeagus spun away from Eros, unable to bear the sympathy in his cousin's eyes. "We were very happy, except for one silly argument, but she would not leave me over that, I'm sure."

Eros coughed. "One silly argument, you say?"

"It wasn't my fault. Pandora was trying to make trouble."

"Oh dear," said Eros, a twinkle in his eye as he threw another grape in his mouth. "This sounds serious if that witch was involved."

Oeagus nodded. "Calliope should have trusted me more. She should have known that I would never ever look at another woman, let alone that liar Pandora."

Eros shook his head. "What exactly did Pandora tell Calliope?"

"She hinted that she and I had been together on my last journey to Thrace. It wasn't true, of course, but since she had been in the traveling party she made it appear to be true."

"Pandora can be very convincing when she puts her mind to it."

Oeagus sighed. "Yes, she can. And it didn't help my case when I forgot to bring a gift back for my lovely wife. I always bring her a gift, but this time I forgot."

"Yes. Well. I can see how Calliope might have gotten the wrong impression. Did you explain to her what really happened?" asked Eros.

"No. That's the terrible thing. She was so angry with me, she didn't give me an opportunity to explain, and then it was too late because she disappeared before I had a chance to convince her it was all a lie."

"Your betrayal of her trust could be a reason for Calliope's loss of memory."

"I did not betray her!"

"But she believes you did, and that is the problem," said Eros.

"Damnation!" Oeagus slammed his fist on the table, scattering the contents of the tray. "What do you suggest I do then? You're supposed to be the expert when it comes to affairs of the heart."

Eros stepped backwards, avoiding the spray from the water jug as it slipped over. "You have to teach her to trust you again."

"But she doesn't even know who I am now. Thanks to my idiocy, she thinks me a lunatic."

"Then you'll just have to work harder," said Eros.

"Can you help?"

Eros grinned. "I can help provide the opportunities, but only you can earn her trust."

Oeagus stood tall and determined. "I will succeed. Failure is not an option."

"Of course you will, my friend. You always win."

* * * *

Gus adjusted the tight clothing he was forced to wear to fit into this strange world. These 'jeans' as Eros called them, were very restrictive, and he found himself wishing for the loose clothing of his kingdom. The material was quite soft and thick, but the design left a lot to be desired. Ahead of him Calliope was walking into a building and he hurried to catch up to her. Eros had told him it was a safe public place to meet, and that many people of this time met up this way. He was not so sure but he entered the edifice anyway. It was a food market of some sort and he was never one to frequent a place of business in the past. He had servants for that. He watched the people there, who all seemed to collect a metal contraption on wheels and push it into the store. He followed suit, checking ahead to make sure he did not lose sight of his quarry.

Calliope headed directly to large crates that displayed fresh fruit and vegetables. Many of them were not familiar to him, but he saw many different varieties of grapes and smiled. *Good, at least that is a food I know I will eat.* He pushed his trolley over to the display so he could pick up a bunch, tasting one of the succulent and juicy spheres.

"You can't eat them until you pay for them, mate," said a woman who stood next to him.

"My apologies," he said. *I will never understand this world.*

She pulled off a soft tissue-like strip of material and handed it to him. "Here, use a bag. I won't tell if you don't," she said as she popped a grape into her own mouth.

He stared at the lightweight bundle she'd given him and wondered what in Hades he was meant to do with it, until he saw her rub the end between her fingers and open one up before throwing bunches of grapes inside. He did the same, quite pleased at his efforts to fit in.

He scanned the rest of the section and noticed Calliope picking up an unfamiliar vegetable and he pushed his trolley over near her.

"Can you tell me the name of that fruit?" he asked.

She jumped. "You!" She turned toward him." What are you doing here?"

He shrugged. "This is a public place, is it not?"

"Yes, but that doesn't explain why you're here. Are you following me?"

He clutched at his chest, pasting the sweetest smile he could find on his face. "You wound me. It was serendipity that brought us to the same place at the same time."

She coughed into her hand. "Sure it was."

"All right, I cannot tell an untruth when I am talking to you. I saw you come in here and I had to see you again."

"I told you yesterday, I've never met you before, I'm not some Greek goddess, and I'm definitely not your wife. I'm sure I'd remember if I was."

"But you admit that you don't remember your earlier life?"

She shifted in her place and spun away from him. "I admit nothing, not that it's any business of yours."

"I'm sorry. I don't mean to frighten you."

She turned back, her eyes narrowed. "You don't scare me. I just want you to leave me alone."

His heart pounded. If he messed this up he might not get another chance to connect with her. "All I'm asking is that you keep an open mind and give me a chance to show you that I mean you no harm."

"Give me one reason why I should do that."

"Because I can help you regain your memory."

She picked up a piece of fruit then rubbed it against her shirt. "What makes you think I have any memory issues?"

He touched her hand and gently traced a line across her soft skin with his index finger. "Yesterday, when I first came across you, you seemed anxious to see if I knew you, almost like you needed to hear it."

Her face colored to a light shade of pink and he smiled. She had blushed just like that for him when he had first courted her.

"I don't remember doing that."

He moved his thumb back and forth over her wrist. "You mouth is saying one thing, but your pulse is telling me another."

She snatched her hand away and massaged the part of her wrist where he had touched her. "You make me nervous, that's all."

He frowned. "I don't want to make you nervous. I want you to like me."

"I don't know you."

"My point exactly. If you get to know me you might like me, just a little."

"I don't think..."

He placed his finger over her lips. "Shh..." he whispered. "What can it hurt if we share a drink in a public place? You can even invite a friend to join us if you want."

She shook her head. "I'm not sure it's a good idea."

"You cannot tell me you are not curious about what I have said?"

"I suppose..."

"Wonderful. It is settled. Can we meet for lunch at the café across the road? You can call your friend to come and join us if you desire it."

"I'll think about it."

"If you wish to discuss this with your friend, go ahead. I will be waiting for you when you are ready."

"All right, but if I'm not there in half an hour I've changed my mind."

"Then I pray to the gods that you don't." He waved before pushing his trolley toward the checkout to pay for his grapes.

"I will see you soon, my love," he whispered as he watched her turn and leave.

Chapter Three

Callie struggled to get her breathing under control, while the man who called himself Gus walked away. She couldn't believe she was actually considering joining him for lunch, but she wanted to find out once and for all if he was a paid actor trying to find his way into the refuge, so for the sake of her friends, she would do it.

If only he wasn't so gorgeous. He took her breath away. And what was that with the major tingles across her skin when he'd touched her?

She couldn't think about that right now, though. The safety of Mardi and everyone at Serenity was at stake.

She finished making her purchases and pulled out her mobile phone to call Mardi, but closed it again. Mardi would only want to come with her, and she really wanted to do this herself. She would make sure there was nothing to fear from this guy and if she could prove someone was paying him to be there, she'd report him to Mardi's boyfriend, Chris. If it turned out he was innocent after all, and just a tiny bit crazy, then no harm no foul.

The breeze picked up while she waited at the corner for the lights to change. Her hair flicked across her face, and she pushed it out of the way only to catch sight of Gus sitting at a table outside the cafe. The sun reflected brightly off his blond hair giving him an angelic appearance, but the heat in his eyes as he stared at her was anything but, and more to the point, why did her body heat all over from that one gaze?

She crossed the street, almost stumbling, but she recovered in time to plaster a confident smile on her face while she sat down opposite Gus. He beamed his megawatt smile at her and she turned away, busying herself by adjusting her chair and moving it a tad farther away from him.

His lips turned up on one corner. "I'm glad you decided to come," he said.

She met his gaze and gave him a wry smile. "I'm not sure why I did, but I'm here now, and I have to eat, so let's get on with it."

He laughed. "There is nothing I would rather do. Shall we order? I'm hungry."

As if by magic a waitress arrived at their side, and judging from the girly giggles she was aiming at Gus, her prompt service wasn't due to Callie being a regular. To her surprise he didn't seem to notice his fan club staring at him. He continued to stare into Callie's eyes, which frustrated the waitress no end, if the expression on her face was anything to go by.

"I am unfamiliar with this food. Can you suggest something for me?"

The waitress opened her mouth to speak, but Gus put his hand up. "Calliope, you must choose for me."

"I must?" she croaked. "I mean..." She swallowed hard as her face warmed. "You want me to order for you?"

He shrugged, giving her another grin. "I am sure whatever you decide will be acceptable."

A muscle twitched on one side of her face and she quickly covered her cheek and faced the waitress. "We'll both have the chicken and avocado focaccia, toasted please, and two cappuccinos."

"Fine. Two daily specials," she said, giving all of her attention to Gus. "Can I get you anything else?"

Oh please – she's practically salivating over him! "Some water would be good."

"Huh?"

Gus took hold of Callie's hand and traced a path over her palm with his thumb. "I believe Callie asked for water."

The waitress cleared her throat and abruptly turned to leave. "Okay, fine. It won't be long."

Callie bit her lip, hiding a smile. "You broke a heart."

"What do you mean?"

She shook her head. "It's obvious she was hanging on your every word. All she wanted was a smile, but you didn't even see her."

He leaned forward and reached out to brush a tendril of her hair behind her ear. "I did not notice."

She shivered. A tingle spread across her scalp and coalesced from her head to her toes.

This has to stop.

If she wasn't careful she would forget the whole reason why she was sitting here with this man who could be a danger to her and everything she held dear.

The best tactic would surely be to ignore his flirting, and since she was not a girl to be distracted from her purpose, or so she thought, she decided to get right to the heart of the matter. "All right, Gus, you promised I could ask you questions."

"Go ahead. Ask me whatever you want. I promise you I will always give you an honest answer."

She blinked, tapping her fingers on the tabletop. "Fine. The first thing you can do is tell me who is paying you to lie to me with all these fanciful stories?"

The smile on Gus' face disappeared. "I do not tell stories, and no one pays me to do anything."

"Come on. Gods and goddesses? Ancient Greek mythology? Please! It has to be a story."

"If you really believe that then why do you respond to me? You cannot deny your heart beats faster in my presence and your skin yearns for my touch."

"It's more that I question your motivation. You confuse me."

"I remind you of what you had before. You are my beloved. I am your husband."

Sweat dampened her skin and her heart did a little dance, kicking this way and that. She couldn't breathe. She felt herself falling backwards and the air around her turned white. Strong hands took hold of her wrists and she heard a voice in the distance.

"Calliope, come back to me…"

She sucked air into her lungs and opened her eyes on a short exhale. Whoa! "What just happened?"

Gus looked concerned as he stared at her from across the table with those eyes as blue as the Aegean Sea. "I'm afraid my words upset you. You were about to faint."

She sat upright and searched for a glass of water. "Where's that waitress? I need water."

Gus held his hand up and the waitress scurried over. "We need water."

Her mouth rounded when she realized her mistake. "I'm sorry, I forgot. I'll get it right away."

"See that you do," he said.

A few seconds later the flustered waitress arrived with a bottle of water and two glasses. "I'm so sorry." She tried pouring the water with her shaking hands but only succeeded in spilling several drops on the table cloth.

Gus released Callie's hands and took the bottle from the waitress, smiling up at her stricken face. "It doesn't matter now. We have the water. I'll pour it."

She gave him a tremulous smile back, nodding and backing away before heading for the kitchen.

Callie took the glass Gus offered her and sipped it slowly. "You certainly have a way of getting people to snap to attention."

He shrugged. "She needed encouragement to improve her performance."

"She'll never forget the water again, that's for sure."

Gus laughed. "Then I have done her a service."

"And for the record — I never faint."

"I know. That is why I am worried about you."

"Don't start with all that again. You don't know me at all."

"I am sorry, I promised I would be honest with you, but it seems my words are just upsetting you."

"Fine. Maybe we should just agree to disagree and leave it at that."

"It is regrettable that you do not believe me. I would like to have a chance to show you that I speak the truth, but at the moment I don't think you are ready for that."

"You got that right!"

The waitress arrived with their meals at that moment, and Callie sighed in relief. "I hope you like chicken and avocado," she said.

"I am certain it will be delicious," said Gus.

Callie thanked the waitress and started cutting into her sandwich. "Mardi brought me here for lunch when I first arrived and it's been my favorite café ever since."

"Mardi is a good friend?"

"She's the best. I don't know where I'd be if I didn't have her."

"Then I am grateful to her."

Gus took a large bite of the sandwich and she couldn't tear her gaze away from his mouth. She had a flashback of sensation, imagining the way his lips moved across her skin. Tempted to slap her own hand to wake up from her dream, she breathed in deeply, letting it out as slowly as she could. "So, what do you think of the food?"

He swallowed and took a sip of water before answering. "It is very different to any I have had before, but I find I like it."

"You've never had chicken and avocado before?"

"Not served in this manner. Placing it between the bread is new to me."

Callie thought back to when she'd first eaten here and realized she'd had the same reaction. Mardi hadn't believed her when she said she'd never eaten a sandwich before. She shrugged. *It doesn't mean he's telling the truth, just because we shared that same experience.*

"I'm sure it won't be the last time then. They can be quite addictive."

He watched her stir her coffee. "What is this drink you have ordered us?"

Now this was getting weird. Mardi had introduced her to coffee too. "Coffee. Actually, a cappuccino. Seriously — you've never had one?"

He took a sip and licked his lips. "Bitter, but delicious. And no, this would be my first time. What is in it?"

"Espresso coffee and frothed milk. It's my favorite way to have coffee."

"I have decided it is my favorite too."

"Have you tried it any other way?"

"No."

She laughed. "Then how can you say it is your favorite?"

"I trust your judgment."

She snorted. "If you don't stop this, I'll start thinking you're a stalker."

He frowned. "You are right. I was never this agreeable before. We disagreed often, although mostly it was friendly banter."

A vision of Gus gripping her shoulders and forcing her to gaze into his eyes flashed across her mind. She didn't want to think about them arguing, or the inevitable passionate make up. She didn't want to think about a life with him at all, past or present. Not until she could trust that he wasn't out to do some harm to the shelter. *Focus on the plan and don't get him off side.* "Not to worry. Let's just enjoy lunch and see what happens."

He grinned. "An excellent idea."

The rest of the meal was relatively silent. Callie couldn't think of any small talk when all she could see as their eyes met was the heat every time she took a bite, and if she were honest, he was making her sweat. The fire in his eyes, the soft touches against her skin while he poured the water or passed the salt, and she was feeling like she'd just run a marathon. After she'd eaten as much as her knotted stomach would let her, she stood up.

"I think I'd better head off now. Thanks for lunch." She held out her hand to him. "Maybe we'll see each other around."

Gus stood and clasped her hand. "I will walk you to your home."

She knew it! He wanted to find the shelter. "That's okay. I'm a big girl. I can make my own way back."

"It will be no trouble."

The waitress arrived with the check and collected the plates. "I hope you enjoyed your meal."

"It was delicious," said Callie. She turned to Gus who was examining the bill. "How much is my share of the check?"

He removed several bills out of his pocket. He placed them on the table. "I will pay for the food."

She picked up half of the money then handed it back to him. "You've overpaid. Here is your change."

He stared blankly at the different colored paper bills she'd placed in his hand. "Thank you. This form of money is difficult to understand."

There he goes again. She'd better escape before she started to believe him.

A cab pulled up in front of the café and she waved at the driver to wait for her. "I'll take the cab, so there's no need for you to walk with me. Thanks again for lunch," she said as opened the passenger door and got in.

The cab drove away and she watched him through the window, standing there staring after her, and her chest tightened.

But I had to do that, she told herself. For the sake of Mardi and the shelter, he can't follow me. *Not when I can't be sure I can believe him.*

* * * *

Mardi frowned at her as she arrived back at Serenity. "You were gone for a long time. Everything okay?"

Callie sighed. "Yes, everything's fine. I had lunch before I came home."

"Are you sure that's it? You seem a little frazzled."

She pressed the bridge of her nose with her thumb and forefingers before taking a breath and letting it out. "Gus showed up again."

"What? He's here?"

"No. He was at the market when I was buying the fruit and veggies. He just appeared."

"That's weird. So is he still insisting you're married?"

"Yes. And he's never had a focaccia before. Or tasted a cappuccino."

"Now that's really weird. Neither had you!"

"Someone must have told him, that's the only explanation."

"Or he's telling the truth?"

"Bite your tongue, Mardi! How could a wild story like that be true? If he is my husband, then that also means I'm a goddess. Last time I looked I didn't have any goddess powers."

"Maybe they don't work here in Australia," she said.

"Mardi! What's gotten into you? You're usually the most logical person around, plus you always want the evidence before you believe anyone."

"I don't know." She giggled. "He's just so gorgeous looking, and it's so romantic, don't you think?"

"Romantic? Who are you and what have you done to Mardi?"

She smiled. "I'm feeling a bit romantic today. So shoot me."

"Is this about Chris? What have you two been up to?"

"Okay. Chris has asked me out to dinner tonight and he says he wants to make it a special night." She grabbed Callie's hand and squeezed. "Oh, my God, I wonder if he's going to propose."

Callie smiled. She liked Chris. The cop had been a great support to Mardi and he definitely adored her. "I hope so. He loves you, so it's not inconceivable that he wants to marry you."

"I know, and I love him too. I just don't want to get my hopes up in case I'm wrong."

"Why don't you take it one step at a time and see how it pans out?"

"I know. I'm trying to be calm about it, but I can't seem to concentrate on the reports I'm writing up."

"So let's go search your wardrobe for something special for you to wear tonight."

"Great idea!"

Callie took Mardi's hand and they walked upstairs toward Mardi's room, only to be stopped by an excited Jack.

"Hey, little man. What's up?"

"I wanna go to the park, but Mummy's got a headache."

Callie glanced at Mardi and lifted an eyebrow.

Mardi nodded. "I'll leave you to get this one, Callie."

"Thanks, friend. I'll be back soon to check on your progress," she replied.

She smiled as her friend continued up the stairs.

Jack grabbed onto her jeans and tugged. "Callie? Can you take me to the park?"

She ruffled his hair. "Only if your mummy says it's okay. Let's go and check on her."

Jack jumped up and down on the spot. "Awesome!"

"Shhh!" said Callie. "Your mum has a headache, remember."

"I forgot," said Jack, whispering loudly as they walked into his room.

Sarah lay on the bed, an arm covering her eyes. Callie went to the window and drew the blinds shut.

Sarah sat up in the bed. "Who is it?"

"Sorry I startled you, Sarah. It's Callie. Jack tells me you have a headache. Is there anything I can do for you?"

She relaxed back onto the pillow. "No, I've had a few ibuprofens. I just need to rest for a bit."

"How about if I take Jack to the park to give you a—?"

"I couldn't ask you to do that."

"Please, Mummy," Jack pleaded.

"I don't mind, Sarah. I promise I'll take care of him."

"All right then. But if it gets too much just bring him back."

Callie laughed. "I'm sure Jack will be on his best behavior. You just take it easy and—"

Jack jumped onto the bed and hugged his mother tightly. "Thanks, Mummy. I love you."

She smiled at her son. "I love you too, Jack. Make me proud by being good for Callie."

"I will, Mummy. I will. I'll be the best boy in the world!"

Callie's heart warmed to watch the interaction with mother and son. How Sarah's husband could be so abusive to those he was supposed to love and care for was beyond her. "I'm sure you will be, Jack. Let's go so your mum's headache can get better."

Jack jumped off the bed, not stopping to catch his breath before he started running to the door.

"Bye, Jack," his mother called after him.

He stopped and turned, waving profusely with his little chubby hand. "Bye, Mummy."

Sarah smiled at Callie gratefully. "Thanks so much."

"No problem at all," she said from where she stood in the doorway. "I'd better hurry and catch him before he's out the front on his own."

Jack appeared in the doorway and tugged at Callie's hand. "Come on! Let's go!"

She closed the door so his mother could sleep in peace. "All right, young man. To the park we go."

After stopping off in Mardi's room to let her know where they were going, she took the mobile phone that Mardi insisted she keep with her when outside, and her keys and purse. They left by the back door and headed toward the back lane.

"I want to go to the park out the window," said Jack.

"We are going there, Jack, but we're going to play a game first. Is that okay?"

"What game?"

"We're going on a treasure hunt. Does that sound like fun?"

"I like treasure."

Callie laughed. "I thought you might."

The first place they went to was a wooden box on the ground under the eaves of the tool shed.

"What's that?" asked Jack.

"Open it and you'll find your first piece of treasure."

Jack didn't need to be told twice. He knelt down to flip open the lid. After a quick look he pulled out a bright yellow Frisbee. His face fell. "What's this for?"

"It's a magical disc. When you throw it, it comes back."

His eyes lit up. "It comes back?"

"Yes, it does. It just takes a bit of practice. I'll show you how when we get to the park."

"Let's go to the park!"

She held out her hand for him to grab a hold. "Okay, young man. Off we go."

His little fingers tightened around hers and he stood up. "Off we go."

There were a number of families at the playground when they arrived, and Callie asked Jack if he wanted to play on the swings or the climbing equipment first, but he shook his head. "I wanna play with the magic disc."

"Magic disc it is then," said Callie.

She walked with him to a large grassed section of the park and scanned the area. There wasn't anyone who they could hit if the Frisbee went awry so it should be pretty safe.

She wrapped her arms around him from behind and showed him the action needed to throw the Frisbee. He flicked his wrist and let go of the toy, but it didn't get very far, rolling around in a circle.

He jumped up and down on the spot, his face beaming. "It came back!"

She smiled at the sound of joy in his voice. He deserved to have more of this, more time to have fun without worrying if his father would hurt his mother. "Well done, little man. You are so clever." She picked up the disc and offered it back to him. "Let's have another try. I'm sure you can do even better this time."

They spent the next half an hour throwing and retrieving the Frisbee, each turn helping Jack to improve his technique, and more importantly, enjoy himself.

"How about we get some ice cream and sit in the sun and watch the ducks at the pond?"

"Yay!" said Jack.

She laughed at his exuberance. "Okay, pick up the Frisbee and we'll head on over to the ice cream shop."

He skipped across to pick it up but stopped still, staring ahead.

"What's up, Jack?"

"Daddy," he whispered.

Callie ran forward and picked him up, drawing him close. Her body went into full alert while she scanned the park area in front of them. "Where is he, sweetie?"

The little boy pointed at a man in the distance who was rushing toward them at breakneck speed.

Oh no! She searched around for the fastest route out of the park and started running. She could feel the little man's heartbeat thumping against her chest where she held him firmly. He gripped her shoulders tightly and hung on as she weaved in and out of the way of other families enjoying their afternoon in the park.

"I'm scared," he whispered in her ear.

"I know, sweetie, but we'll be okay."

"My daddy is angry. He hurts my mummy when he's angry."

"Don't worry. We'll hide from him and he won't be able to find us." She took a quick glance behind her and saw him still coming fast at them. She really hoped she was telling Jack the truth and they would get away, but she didn't like their chances at the moment.

Up ahead she saw an opportunity when the tram at the corner rang the bell, signaling it was about to leave. She ran as fast as she could and made it up the stairs just before the doors closed. The tram pulled away but Jack's father reached the door and thumped on it, shouting at the driver to let him in.

Callie's heart pounded. She prayed the driver would ignore his angry pleas. Jack shivered as he burrowed into her neck. She stroked his back, soothing him while she waited to see what happened next. She jumped as a man sat down beside her and leaned over to speak to her.

"What do you think you're doing?" she shouted at the large figure.

"Calliope, I am here to help you," said a familiar voice.

She turned and scrutinized the man at her side. "Gus? How the heck did you get here?"

"Don't worry about that. I will make sure that man does not continue to follow you."

The door began to open as the man in the street ran to get in.

"How are you going to do that?"

He turned and lifted his hand, and it changed direction and shut again. Jack's father bashed against the tram, obscenities pouring from his mouth. The tram moved off and in seconds they were halfway up the street, some distance from danger, at least temporarily.

Callie gaped at Gus in awe. "What did you do?" If he'd stopped Jack's father, that was great, but that didn't explain how he happened to be on the tram, and it certainly didn't allay her suspicions that he was working for Jack's father.

He smiled at her, a small dimple appearing in his left cheek. "We don't have time for explanations now. He could follow us, so we need to get out of here and lose him once and for all."

She did need to get off the tram, and if he could help achieve that, she'd take that chance. As long as he didn't find Serenity, they'd be fine. "You won't get any argument from me. But I won't forget what you did, and I will be asking."

He laughed. "Of course you will. You would not be Calliope if you didn't. "

Jack turned and smiled at Gus. "Who are you, mister?"

"I'm a friend of Calliope's"

"Who's Call-eye-pee?"

"He means me, Jack."

"Her name's Callie."

He smiled. "All right, I'll call her Callie just for you then." He reached out and touched Callie's shoulder. "We'd better get off. Do you want me to carry the child?"

Callie tightened her grip on Jack. "No. I'm fine."

He narrowed his eyes, but he didn't comment.

The tram slowed down before it stopped on a screech of brakes.

"Follow me closely."

She nodded. They didn't have any other choice.

Gus led them through a shop front and out to a back lane where they found a taxi waiting. *How did he do that?*

He opened the door then extended his arms to take Jack from her, but again she refused his help. She slipped into the back seat with Jack on her lap and waited for him to join them, but to her surprise he closed the door and spoke to the driver, giving him a wad full of cash.

She opened the window and called out to him. "You're not coming with us?"

"Not this time, Calliope. I sense you don't trust me yet, so it is better if you find your way to safety without worrying that I am out to get something from you."

She felt both relief that he was showing her she could trust him, and disappointment that he wasn't coming with them, because if she was truthful, she was drawn to him. "That's very noble of you, Gus. Thanks. I guess I'll be seeing you around?"

He smiled at her and winked. "You can count on it. Be safe, my love."

As the taxi drove off, she turned and watched him as he raised his hand and saluted.

What am I going to do about him?

Chapter Four

Gus paced back and forth in his hotel suite while he waited for Eros. He fought the urge to find that man who was following Calliope and the child and banish him to the fires of Hades, but he knew that wouldn't work in this world. He didn't need to attract attention to himself while he tried to fit in and regain the trust of his wife. He squeezed his fists tight, remembering the look of terror on that little boy's face, and the fear in Calliope's eyes. He wanted to protect her and he damn well would.

The door opened and Eros strode in. His full-length leather coat swished back and forth and squeaked as he lazed across the back of the couch. "Hey, bro—whazzup?"

"Excuse me?"

Eros laughed. "I asked you what the problem is. Get with the program!"

"I'm not sure what program you're talking about, but I need your help."

"Jeez Louise, you're so tightly sprung sometimes. I swear it's a miracle we're such good friends."

"Normally your antics amuse me, cousin, but this time more than ever we both need to be serious."

Eros took a step closer to Oeagus. "What can I do? Is it Calliope?"

"She's in danger and I need help to keep her safe."

Eros jumped back and forth, his fists clenched as he punched the air. "What? Let me at them!"

"Don't worry. I will make sure the culprit suffers, but I need to do it in the ways of this land. I can't draw attention to myself, or to Calliope."

"True. And you can't just whisk her back to Mount Olympus or she might not ever remember. I see your dilemma." He narrowed his eyes. "What can I do?"

"I need to find out more about this place where my wife lives, and the people she helps there. Specifically about the man who tried to abduct her and a young child from a park today."

"The vilest of beasts! I'll see what I can find out. I'll ask Morpheus. I'm sure he'll be able to help."

"Good. In the meantime I have decided to keep a closer eye on Calliope and the house where she lives."

"Won't that make her suspicious of your motives? She does not trust you."

"I will keep hidden until an opportunity arises. Her safety is more important at the moment. Once this danger is passed, perhaps she will allow me to help her regain her memories."

Eros stepped forward and hugged him, slapping him on the back before stepping back. "She will remember. A love such as the one you both share will never die."

Gus smiled sadly. "I know this is true of me, but what if Calliope does not want to remember?"

"Don't even think that way, Oeagus. Whatever walls she has built to block out her memories, I am confident you will find a way to tear them down and bring her back to you."

"I hope so, my friend. I really hope so. And soon."

Eros flashed him a cheeky grin. "Besides, my prophecy tells me together you will have two sons. So hurry up and get started."

"If I was not so worried about the current situation, I would take comfort from that, but the way things stand, I am skeptical that will happen. But I thank you for trying to cheer me up, my friend."

"Have my prophecies ever been wrong in the past?"

Gus laughed. "Yes."

"All right, so I thought Hera and Zeus would be a love match. Everyone is entitled to one mistake."

"A pretty big mistake."

"Agreed, but I was only a child then. I've had a lot more success since that disaster."

"Let's hope so." He picked up his room key card then slipped it in his pocket. "Have you exchanged my gold for the money of this land?"

"Oh yes," he said. He pulled out a wad of paper from the pocket of his leather coat before handing it to Gus. "Here it is. Don't flash it around. In this world flashing your money around not only attracts too much attention, but it is a sure-fire way to be robbed."

Gus stuffed the cash into the pocket of his jeans. "Thank you for the warning. I'll try to remain inconspicuous."

Eros nodded. "And I'll get that information for you and return."

"I'll be watching over Calliope, so you will have to find me."

Eros winked. "I found her the first time, didn't I?"

"That you did. And I am forever in your debt."

"Hey, that's okay. Calliope is like a sister to me. I'd do anything for her."

"Thank you, my friend. Now go and speak to Morpheus."

"Bossy as always," he said, lifting his hand and waving it in a circle.

When he disappeared, Gus could still hear him singing some song about sweet dreams, which gave him an idea. He waved his hand and followed his friend.

* * * *

Callie and Mardi were sitting in the kitchen with Sarah when Chris knocked on the back door. Mardi opened it to him, kissing him on the mouth before he walked inside. Sarah cringed at the sight of his police uniform.

Callie reached over and clasped Sarah's freezing hand from where it rested on the table. "Don't worry. He's a friend. He's here to help us."

Her shoulders relaxed a little, but she didn't return the smile he gave her.

"You must be Sarah. I'm Chris." He was an imposing figure, with his buzz-cut auburn hair and massive shoulders. He held out his hand but she didn't take it.

Instead she increased her grip on Callie's fingers. "I don't know what you can do. I've never been able to get the police to stop Adam before. No one believes me."

Chris pulled out the remaining chair so he could sit down opposite Sarah. "I believe you. Can you tell me your story from the beginning?"

She smirked. "Not much use in doing that. He always managed to put on a good show to make out I was the crazy one. You won't find any record of my complaints against him."

"You're right. I couldn't find anything. Which is strange. Why do you think that is?"

"It's probably because he used to be a cop."

Chris leaned back against the chair and rubbed a hand over his spiky hair. "Shit."

"Now you can see why you can't help me? None of his mates would put any of the reports in," said Sarah.

He sat forward. "Did you try taking out an intervention order, or an Apprehended Violence Order?"

"What's the use of an AVO? He thinks he's bulletproof. No one was going to arrest him. Adam was very clever making sure none of my bruises showed outside of my clothes."

Chris stood and paced back and forth. "What a bastard."

Mardi placed her hand on Sarah's shoulder. "We've seen creeps like him before. We know how clever they can be."

Chris poured some water into a glass he took out of the cupboard over the sink. "Yeah, but it's just wrong that fellow cops are covering up for one of them. What's his full name?"

"Adam Simpson. He used to be stationed at Brunswick CID."

"Shit. I know him. He's a prick. I can totally believe he's doing this."

"I don't want to press charges. I just want to be free of him."

Callie felt sick. How could a man who's supposed to love and protect his family turn so violent, then enlist the help of others to hide his sins? This was truly evil at its worst. She released Sarah's hand and rose from her chair, moving to the sink to fill the kettle before turning it on. "I'll make us all some calming tea so we can think clearly on what we're doing."

Sarah smiled weakly. "Thanks so much, Callie. I'm so sorry for what he put you through today."

Chris turned to Callie. "What did he do to you? I only heard that he might be following Sarah and her son."

"I was in the park with Jack, and his father came toward us. I grabbed Jack and ran the other way. Luckily there was a tram waiting on the corner and we jumped on just before it drove off. We lost him after that."

"How did he find you at the park?"

"You know, I didn't think about that. I have no idea. We took the long way to get there too." Callie closed her eyes and thought about Gus and her suspicions that he was working with Sarah's husband. Despite the fact that he'd helped them to escape, he had appeared out of nowhere. Had he followed her home yesterday? She hoped not, because she really wanted to believe that he was just a gorgeous, albeit slightly crazy man who seemed to be interested in her.

Mardi stood behind Chris and rubbed his shoulders. "I think I know. There are closed circuit cameras in that park now. If Adam is a cop, he could possibly get access to the films, or he might even have Jack's picture out there."

Sarah paled. "He has a friend who works in the roads and traffic department."

Chris keyed in a number on his phone. "George. Chris Watson here. How's it going? Good, good here. Yeah, mate, just a quick question. Do you have an alert on the CCTV's for a missing child?" He paced the room, nodding and grunting at the person on the other end of the conversation. "You'll let me know if anything shows up? Thanks, mate."

Chris sat back down while Callie placed the teapot and mugs on the bench and joined them at the table.

"George is a friend of mine in Traffic. He says he doesn't know anything about a BOLO for a missing child."

"So it can't be the cameras ", said Callie.

"Not necessarily," said Chris. "Adam might have asked his mates to do it on the quiet."

"That's something he would do," said Sarah. "He hates anyone knowing his business."

"I just had another idea," said Mardi. "We thought he was following us when we picked up Sarah and Jack the day before yesterday. I thought I'd lost him in the traffic, but maybe he got my number plate. With his contacts he could have done a search on the car registration."

Callie poured Chris a cup. "That's a possibility. He got close enough for us to read his plates, so it stands to reason he could read ours."

Chris smiled his thanks and took the cup. "True, however that doesn't explain how he found you in the park."

"It's not such a stretch. It's in the next street. He could have taken a punt that Sarah would take Jack to the park."

"Yeah, but he got you instead. Lucky you're such a quick thinker and managed to get away."

She thought again of Gus and how he'd somehow made the door of the tram close and the driver move on. Surely it was just a coincidence. That's what she told herself when she decided not to share that little snippet of information. It had to be, otherwise he might not be as mad as she thought. Plus that made her a goddess, and she knew she had no magical powers of her own.

"Callie?"

She broke out of her reverie to find Mardi staring at her expectantly. "Yes? Sorry, did I miss something?"

"Chris suggested we all stay inside for a few days. He's going to keep watch on the house and co-opt a few mates to help out. Are you okay with that?"

"But what about your date tonight?"

Mardi sighed. "We've rescheduled for next week."

"I'm so sorry, Mardi. I know how excited you were about it."

"The safety of everyone here is more important. We'll have someone watching the house at all times. How does that sound?"

"That sounds reasonable." She certainly wasn't ready to be confronted by an angry husband again, but a part of her was hoping to find Gus and get him to explain how he'd done whatever it was he'd done to help her and Jack escape in the park. *Never mind.* She could catch him up later on. If he really was her husband, he wouldn't be going anywhere in a hurry.

Sarah stood. "I don't know how to thank you all. I feel so bad to have put you all in danger." Her face crumpled and tears flowed down her cheeks.

Callie wrapped her arms around her. "That's why we're here, Sarah. That's why Serenity exists. You and Jack finding a safe new life makes it all worth it."

* * * *

Callie tingled all over. She was floating on the softest of beds and warm hands were sliding delicately over her skin, sending quivers everywhere they touched. Her eyes stayed closed and she smiled while she lifted her arms as her lover slipped her T-shirt over her head.

"Beautiful," he whispered. "I missed you, my love."

He's back. *"Who are you?"*

"Someone who loves you," he said.

Clever fingers tweaked at her nipples, pinching just enough to send sparks directly to her core. He slipped one of his hands under the elastic of her boxers, where she was already wet, writhing and wanting more, and she gasped. Her pajama bottom went the way of her top and in an instant she was naked. She shivered at the cool breeze tickling her skin. She opened her legs and his warm body moved up between them, covering her with a burning heat while his mouth latched on to her breast and she thrashed her head from side to side. The sensations intensified when her lover moved down, grasping her hips as he licked her folds from top to bottom. A finger entered her and her muscles squeezed tightly around it. Oh my goddess! *She was rewarded when he inserted another digit and kept up the sensual torture.*

Her dream lover continued his carnal assault on her body, his fingers twisting and turning and sending her nerve endings into a frenzy. As much as she tried, she couldn't see his face, but his body was perfection. All muscle and smooth skin. He entered her, filling her to the core. She cried out and he claimed her mouth, devouring her and taking her breath away.

Her breathing was erratic as he moved in and out, gradually increasing his pace. He played her like a violin until the sensations became too much and she flew over the edge, calling out a name she couldn't remember.

Afterwards he kissed her gently and smoothed her hair off her face before he left.

She drifted back into a deep dreamless sleep, her body relaxed and sated.

When the sun woke her, refreshed and smiling she threw back her sheets and sat up.

Oh, my goddess! She spied her pajamas in a pile on the floor and drew the sheet back to cover her nakedness. She never slept in the nude. Ever.

She rubbed her hand quickly over her body, finding her nipples tender and dampness between her legs. *It was a dream, wasn't it?* People didn't have sex in their sleep. They'd wake up for sure, wouldn't they? Especially sex with such an emotional connection like she'd just had. *It had to be a dream.* A product of her imagination, of course. There was no reason for her to think of Gus, but she was sure it was him. *Was it his name I called?* She didn't know if this was a memory or a reaction to all the events of the day. She tried to put it out of her mind as she pulled on her pajamas and jumped out of her bed, but that was nigh impossible when she straightened the sheets and inhaled the scent of musk and sex. It must have been an amazing dream for her to have orgasmed in her sleep. The only problem was, she didn't yet trust the person who'd caused them. Or did she?

Chapter Five

Gus pulled the collar of his jacket up and shoved his hands in his pockets as he walked the perimeter of Calliope's block. He'd tied his hair back with a leather strip and he hoped it was enough to make him less recognizable. This would be his fifth circuit of the neighborhood and so far it was all quiet. No sign of the man who threatened his beloved. In fact, no one had left in the five hours since he'd been standing watch, and the only person who had visited was a policeman who was apparently involved with the blonde woman who lived with Calliope. He noticed the policeman had his own precautions in place, spying another car park across the street with the driver remaining inside, apparently settling in for surveillance. If he hadn't seen that same policeman walk over to the car and speak to the driver, he would have been alarmed. This time was obviously a changing of the guard. The first cop spoke for a few minutes to the second cop before leaving. It was good to know Calliope's new friends were taking turns to watch over them, but he still needed to do it himself, for his own peace of mind.

He took a chance and stared up at the house, hoping to catch a glimpse of Calliope, and wondering what she was thinking about this morning. He hoped she had started to remember something of their life together. It was difficult seeing her and having her treat him like a complete stranger. He craved her like no other woman, but he couldn't give in to the urge to whisk her away right now. Her safety was more important, and as Akeso, the great healer had said, she could not be forced, or it could be dangerous. If a goddess was forced to confront a memory they did not wish to, it could send them into fugue state, from which they may never recover. He would die first, rather than be the cause of that. At least he was here and could make sure nothing happened to her. He didn't care how long it took, even if his generals called him back to the throne. He wouldn't go. Calliope was his priority and he was staying right here until he was convinced she was safe and happy. His heart ached to think she might never regain her memory. He would fight for her, but he had to accept that in the end he could end up saying goodbye, because her happiness meant more to him than his desire to claim her. And if he pushed too hard, it could have disastrous consequences. Either way he would continue to keep watch over her, even if it was through Eros. Hopefully it wouldn't come to that.

A sudden movement at an upstairs window caught his eye. It was only a flash, but he was pretty sure he recognized the long, dark flowing hair. A few seconds later his thoughts were confirmed when she came storming out of the front door and marched across the road directly to where he was standing.

"What in Hades are you doing here, Gus?"

The cop doing the surveillance flew out of his car and caught up with them, his hand hanging loosely in front of the gun he had holstered at his hip. "Is this man bothering you, ma'am?"

She shook her head. "Yes, but not the way you think."

Gus put his hands up. "I'm only here to make sure that evil man does not return and try to take you away again."

The cop took a step closer. "Hey, do you want me to get rid of him?"

Callie stood her ground. "No, it's fine. I can handle him."

He relaxed his hand and turned to leave. "Okay, but if he gives you any trouble just yell and I'll be back."

"Thanks, Officer, I've got it."

Gus watched him until he got back in his car and closed the door. "I am sorry if I alarmed you, Calliope. That was not my intention."

She narrowed her eyes. "How did you find me? I'm confused. How do you know where I live? Have you taken up stalking me now?"

"You are not my prey. I am merely concerned for your welfare, especially after what happened yesterday."

"Nice deflection, but you didn't answer my question. How did you find me?"

He smiled. "You won't believe me. You already think I am delusional."

"Try me."

"Eros told me."

"Who is Eros?"

"The God of Love, and your cousin."

She sighed. "You don't give up, do you? Making up fantastic stories is only cute for a little while. This is serious now, so you need to tell me the truth."

"I did say you wouldn't believe me, but I do speak the truth."

"Prove it then."

He took her hand. "Fine, but we need to be somewhere more private to continue this conversation."

"I'm not taking you inside."

He slipped his hand in hers. "That will not be a problem. We can have another one of those cappuccinos you are so fond of."

"Okay, but I need to tell Mardi what I'm doing."

"Mardi?"

"My friend. We work together and share the house."

"Ah…I remember now. I have much to thank her for."

She looked at him sideways and untangled her hand from his. "Sure you do." She dug into her pocket for her mobile phone before tapping in a number. "Mardi? I'm heading out for coffee with Gus." She held her phone away from her ear.

Gus heard a loud squeal coming from the phone.

"Yes, that Gus…yes, I'll be fine. Yes, I'll be back soon. Fine. Okay, good. See you." She finished her call and stood to attention. "Let's get this over with then."

He smiled at her. She was very endearing when she was annoyed. "It will not be a trial."

"I just want to get some answers."

"And I will give them to you."

They walked the two blocks to the café in silence. Calliope didn't seem in the mood for small talk so he allowed her time to digest what he had already told her. Maybe she would believe him, or at the very least, believe that he meant her no harm.

They sat in a booth inside the café, as he did not want to chance that she would be seen. Once they'd ordered he placed his hands on the table and leaned forward.

"Ask me anything. I have said before, I will answer you truthfully."

"Talk is cheap. I want proof. Show me the evidence that what you say is the truth."

He sighed. He could not put on too much of a show here without drawing attention to them. "Do you remember what you saw in the tram yesterday?"

"You mean the door thing? I figured that was the tram driver."

He laughed. "You have rationalized it in your mind. You did not think that at the time. Tell me honestly, what did you think when you saw the door closing?"

She flushed and turned away. "I don't remember what I thought. It was twenty-four hours ago."

Fine. If that was the way she wanted to do this, he would go along with her—for now. He lifted his hand and waved it over the sugar bowl in front of her. It tipped over and the sugar packets spilled out over the paper tablecloth.

Her eyes widened. "That's a good magic trick. I saw a magician do that on the television the other night."

"You can do it too."

"No I can't!"

He stared into her eyes, seeing the fear and uncertainty there. "Yes. You can. You need to relax and concentrate and it will happen."

He picked up her hand and supported it around the wrist, holding her palm over the sugar bowl.

"Concentrate. See it moving in your head. You can do it.

Her hand shook as he held it in place and she closed her eyes.

When nothing happened immediately, she took her hand back. "This is silly. I can't do this."

"You can, but you are not ready to believe it, so I will not push you. It will come in time."

Calliope twisted a strand of her hair around her finger tightly. "You're mad."

The waitress arrived and they both sat silently while their coffee was placed in front of them. The minute she left Calliope spoke again. "I haven't seen any of this proof you promised me. I've given you the benefit of the doubt up until now, but now it's time for me to ask you some questions and you must give me truthful answers. None of this magic and ancient Greek stuff. Just the truth."

Gus broke eye contact and covered his face with his hands. This was going to be more difficult than he thought, and he needed to tread carefully. Plan A hadn't worked and he didn't really have a plan B at the moment. Plan C, the desperation plan was looking more attractive as the seconds ticked by. "Ask away. I have always promised to tell the truth and I don't plan to go back on that now."

Callie tapped her fingers on the table. "I don't know how else to ask this question, so I'll just blurt it out."

"Go ahead."

She turned her face to the side and back, refusing to meet his eyes. "Did someone pay you to get close to me?"

His chest tightened at her words. "You have asked that before. The answer is still no. Why would anyone want to do that?"

"So no one wanted to find out where I live and asked you to follow me?"

He shook his head. "No, absolutely not. I already told you how I found you."

She raised her hand. "Stop. I told you none of that gods and goddesses stuff."

He swallowed a laugh. She had no idea what he was capable of. Maybe it was time to show her. He leaned forward again and gently grasped her hands. "Close your eyes."

She tugged, but he held fast. "Why?"

He squeezed her fingers slightly and rubbed his thumbs over her palms. "Humor me."

He reached for her and gently kissed her lips. Her eyelids fluttered and closed. It was a mere touch, but heat surged through his body. His hunger for her rose, however he knew he needed to hold back. There would be time for that later. For now he needed her to trust him. Their lips locked together, and they breathed in each other's essence as they kissed. They rose as one above the table, through the roof and into the sky. The wind whispered through Calliope's hair and it swirled, circling both of their bodies. He poured all his love into that one touch and lifted them higher until they floated above the city. Soft flower petals whirled around them. He ended the kiss and moved back, staring at his wife as she followed him with her lips, urging him to continue the kiss, but he resisted. He knew how she felt, but this was not the time to overwhelm her.

"Open your eyes, my beloved."

She smiled dreamily and opened first one, then the other before grasping his hands firmly and letting out an almighty scream. "What...what?"

He held her elbows to steady her. "Do not worry, my love. You are safe with me."

"B...but how? What?"

He couldn't remember ever seeing her this tongue-tied. "No, you are not imagining it. We are flying."

She tightened her grip on his wrists, pulling herself closer to him. "Is this a trick?"

He shook his head. "No trick, my love. I am a demi-god, and you are a goddess. We come from an ancient land."

Her mouth opened and a myriad of emotions crossed her face. "Then that means..."

"Yes, you are my wife. I am your husband."

She closed her eyes. "Take me back down."

"I tell the truth."

"I believe you, but I need to be on terra firma."

He nodded, and they parted as they glided back to their seats.

Calliope scanned one side of the restaurant to the other before leaning forward in her seat. "Why is no one staring at us?" she whispered.

"They did not see us move. For all they know we were still sitting here drinking our coffee."

"Thank goodness. I would hate to end up on the evening news."

"I would not like that either. It is best not to draw too much attention to us when we are in a strange land."

"You're in a strange land. I am in my home."

"You have only been here for six months."

"But it feels like my home."

"Does it? Or do you not search for something else? Your true home?"

She opened her mouth then closed it again.

"You see, I speak the truth."

"If you are my husband, why am I here? And why don't I remember you?"

"I believe you were banished from your home by the actions of your father's jealous wife."

"What did I do to upset her?"

"Nothing. Your father loves your mother and does not love his wife. It is not your fault."

"That's sad. So who is my father again?" Her hands were shaking as she picked up her cup and took a sip.

"Zeus. The King of the Gods."

Callie coughed, almost choking on her drink.

Gus stood up, going to her and rubbing her back. "Are you all right, my love?"

"I'm fine. I'm trying to digest the fact that I'm the daughter of Zeus."

"It is true," he said, returning to his seat.

"You haven't answered my other question either. Why don't I remember you?"

"Alas, that I cannot answer, my love. I wish I could."

She turned away, staring at a spot on the tablecloth. "You tell me all of this, but for all I know we aren't even married. You could be an enemy of my father, trying to elicit your revenge."

He laughed. "Believe me, if I were your enemy, I would have captured you and taken you back to my mountain by now. You would not be here, free to roam as you please."

She stared back at him. "Okay then. If we have such a good marriage, why can't I remember the love of my life? Did you do something to lose my trust?" She covered her mouth with her hand and gasped. "Or did I do something?"

He shifted in his place. He wanted to be completely honest with her but did not want to tell her of their problems until she trusted him. "You have never done anything to damage our relationship, my love."

"Then it was you."

"I didn't say that. We had a misunderstanding, but we had worked it out before you disappeared."

She arched an eyebrow. "A misunderstanding? It must have been a big one if that's why I can't remember my life."

"It was nothing. Just a disagreement."

"From the way you are squirming I can see it was more than a disagreement."

He shrugged. "I speak the truth, but I have already told you more than I should. The healers have said it is better if you remember on your own."

"Forget what they say. I need to know."

"I cannot. I have already said too much, but I wanted you to trust me."

She snorted. "Trust? After what you've just said? It might take me a bit of time, even if I do believe you, and I'm still not sure if I do. For all I know you slipped something into my drink."

He touched her hand, savoring the softness of her skin before she pulled it away. "I would never do that. Please believe this one thing. I love you above all others."

"I'm not convinced of that yet. At least answer me this one question. If you love me as much as you say, and have all these powers, why did it take six months to find me?"

He turned his head and sighed. "I searched our own lands day and night. I did not suspect Hera would send you to another dimension. It was only when Eros visited his favorite land that he picked up your scent."

"Fine. Okay." She stood abruptly. "I think I've heard enough for one day. I need to go home."

He beamed at her. "I can take you there now."

She held her hand up. "No, not there. I'm not convinced I believe all of this yet. I meant back to Serenity. I have a lot of information to digest."

He got out of his chair and walked toward her. "I will accompany you."

"No, I'd rather you didn't."

"You forget—there is a threat to you and your friends. I will see you safely back to them."

"Really, you don't need to do that. I need some distance right now."

He waited while she pushed her chair under the table. "I can be silent while we walk, however I will keep you safe. Believe this one thing. You are my life, and I can do no less."

She crossed her arms in front of her. "Fine. Whatever. But I'm holding you to the not talking bit."

"I promise."

She moved past him and out to the street, and he watched her walk gracefully in front of him. Calliope took his breath away even here in this strange land. He decided that these 'jeans' would become regular clothing for her when they returned to their home. He shook his head, annoyed that he'd allowed himself to be distracted. He picked up the pace, scanning both sides of the street before catching up with her. He stopped himself from remarking that she should remain on the inside of the pathway so he could protect her better. He would keep a closer eye out for potential threats instead. A promise was a promise and he would not disappoint her now. He would give her some time to remember, and he had to believe she would. Their love was meant to be. Hopefully it wouldn't take much longer.

* * * *

Callie rubbed her temples. The headache wasn't helped by the legion of information flying around inside her head. What if everything Gus had said was true? In her heart she knew he spoke the truth as he knew it, but was it also *her* truth? She heard the laughter of young Jack as he played with Mardi in the lounge room, and it reminded her of her current priorities. She didn't have time to deal with Gus right now. They had more important issues to contend with. Like Sarah's violent husband.

She placed her bag on the counter and straightened up, wiping her damp hands against her jeans before she joined the others. She smiled at Jack, who was playing a simple card game with her friend. Nothing like watching children having fun to help her to forget her own troubles for a few minutes.

Jack's delighted squeal rang through the room. "Snap!"

"You beat me again," said Mardi, her eyes twinkling. "You're just too good at this."

He giggled as he swept up his winning pack of cards. "If you play again you might get better," he said. "You might even beat me!"

Callie stifled the laugh that bubbled up in her chest before she spoke solemnly to the Jack. "That's right. Mardi needs a lot of practice to beat a champion like you."

His chest puffed out and his face beamed. "You wanna play, Callie?"

She shook her head quickly and held her hands up. "Oh no. Mardi needs to play again. I'll just watch."

Mardi shot her a 'thanks for nothing' face and picked up her pile. "I'll have you know there are other games where I'm considered a champion."

"I'm sure there are, but since you're doing such a great job here, why stop now?"

"Sure. Your lame attempt at flattery might work better if you get us some refreshments. I'll have a cup of tea." She smiled at Jack. "What would you like, little man?"

"Juice!"

"No problem. I'll be right back. I'll get one for Sarah too. Is she okay?"

"She's doing some laundry. She's trying to keep busy."

"I'll find her and ask her. She might need some company."

Jack and Mardi were wrapped up in the game again when she left the room and searched for Jack's mother. She found her in the back garden hanging out wet clothes on the rickety wire clothes line they'd been meaning to replace once more funding came through. Maybe she could use these powers she was supposed to have to fix it? She'd ask Gus when she next saw him.

Sarah turned as she approached. Her body tensed and she lowered her head. "I'm sorry if I've done the wrong thing. I was trying to be helpful."

Callie wrapped her arms around the smaller woman and hugged her tightly. "You've done nothing wrong. That evil man has made you lose all your self-confidence. You have to remember that you are a wonderful person and a fantastic mother. Don't let him take that away from you."

"In my head I know this, but it's hard when I've had years of being in trouble for everything I do. It's a tough habit to break."

"I know it is. It takes time. He's done his work well, but we'll help you get past it." She released her but kept one arm draped around her shoulder. "I'm making a cup of tea. Come and join us."

Sarah pointed to the basket of wet clothes at her feet. "But the washing?"

"It can wait. Besides, we probably should stay inside the house, remember."

Sarah covered her mouth with her hand. "Oh no! I forgot!"

"Don't worry. It's probably fine and we have Chris' police friends keeping an eye on the house, but to be on the safe side let's stay inside until we know a little more."

"I'm so sorry to put you all in danger."

"Stop right there," she said, putting her hand up. "We do this all the time, and we do it because we want to help people like you and Jack. We wouldn't do it otherwise. So stop worrying."

"Okay. It's just hard, you know. No one has ever done this much for me before without wanting something in return."

"We do want something in return."

Her mouth opened. "What?"

"We want you safe and happy. That's why we do it."

"How can I ever thank you?"

"Just move on with your life and never go back."

"That's what I want too."

"Then that's what you'll do. Never forget you are an amazing woman, and you have the power to do anything."

"You make it sound so easy."

"It is, once you throw off all the negative energy and concentrate on the good things you want in your life."

She gave her a shaky smile. "Thank you. I feel better now. Let's get that cup of tea you mentioned."

"Yes, we'd better do that before Mardi sends out a search party for hers. She can get ugly when she doesn't have her tea."

Sarah laughed while they walked into the house together. "Now that I'd like to see."

"It's not pretty!"

"I guess not. So what can I do to help?"

Callie opened the fridge and pulled out a few pieces of fruit. "How about you slice it up, and I'll make the drinks. We may as well make it a healthy snack while we're at it."

Sarah turned on the tap and started washing the produce. "That's a lovely idea. Jack loves apples and strawberries."

"I'm rather partial as well. I could eat them all day."

"So could Jack."

The kettle boiled, and Callie seared the teapot before spooning in the leaves. "Mardi would never forgive me if we used tea bags."

"I'd never forgive you for what?"

"Ouch!" Sarah clutched her finger and rushed to the sink. Blood dripped from a deep cut, spilling down the sides of her hand and into the drain.

Mardi rushed to her side. "I'm so sorry. I must have startled you. Let me see."

"It's my fault. I'm really clumsy."

"It's no one's fault. Just an accident." Callie opened the cupboard over the sink and pulled out the first-aid kit.

Mardi opened it, collecting a few large gauze swabs and started cleaning the wound.

Jack ran into the room, heading for Sarah. "Mummy!"

Callie turned and picked up the anxious little boy, stroking his back. "Your mummy is fine. She just cut herself. We'll fix it."

"I'm thinking we might need a bit of extra help here. It's quite deep. Can you get my car keys?" Mardi asked Callie. "I'll have to take Sarah to the ER, I think."

Jack started to cry. "I wanna go with my mummy!"

Sarah tensed. She sighed, as if the weight of the world was on her shoulders.

Callie intervened. "No, sweetheart. You stay here with me so that Mardi can get your mummy fixed quicker. They won't be long and we can play some more games."

Sarah flashed her a grateful smile. "That's right, Jack. Callie will stay with you and I'll be home before you know it."

Mardi wrapped Sarah's hand firmly in a bandage and grabbed her bag from the coat rack. "We'll slip out the back and take the scenic route. I'll call you when we get there. Don't forget to keep the doors locked."

Callie held open the back door for them. "Don't worry about us. Chris has his mates watching the house. We're safe. Just get that hand attended to."

"We'll be back as soon as we can."

Callie smiled at Sarah, hoping her calm demeanor would help her not to worry about Jack. "Take as long as you need." She turned to Mardi. "And drive safely!"

"Don't I always?"

"Of course you do. That's why I reminded you."

Mardi laughed, her hand jiggling the keys as she went out the door. "One day I'll get you back for your total lack of faith." She blew her a kiss before closing the door behind her.

Callie locked the door and slid the bolt into place. Her smile froze when she turned back to Jack and saw his face. The brave little man's bottom lip wobbled as he struggled to stop himself from crying. She crossed the floor and picked him up, cradling his head against her shoulder. She whispered to him. "It's okay, Jack. Your mummy will be fine. It might take a while because the hospital is sometimes slow, but don't worry. She'll be back here as soon as you can say 'Jack Robinson'."

Jack lifted his head back and looked at her. "My name isn't Jack Robinson! It's Jack Simpson."

"I know, sweetie. It's just an expression."

"What's a 'spression?"

Callie stifled a grin. "It's just something people say to help make something sound fun."

"Like a story?"

She laughed. "Yes, like a story, I guess."

"I love stories. Can you tell me a story, Callie?"

Sure. She could do that. Stories were her specialty. "No problem, sweetie. Let's get comfortable and I'll tell you the best story you've ever heard."

"Awesome!"

Thank the goddess calming him down had been easy. The poor little mite had been through a lot in his short life. She carried him into the lounge room and sat down on the couch.

"Okay, gorgeous boy, let's start the story. Which one do you want to hear?"

"Tell me the one about the king again!"

"All right. The king it is."

She gave Jack a few minutes to fidget and get comfortable before she started.

"Once upon a time there was a giant king who lived in a faraway place. He was the strongest man in the land and all his enemies were afraid of him. One day he felt lonely and decided to find a new friend, so he traveled across the sea in a big boat to another kingdom and started looking."

"Oh—I love boats!"

"So do I," she said, smiling. "Do you want to hear the rest of it?"

"Yes!"

"Okay. Where were we? Oh yes—when the king reached the other kingdom he was invited to a big party by the king of the new land. There were hundreds of people there and lots of the best foods and desserts."

"Chocolate?"

She laughed. "Yes, there was chocolate. And cake, and fruit and juice."

"Juice! I love juice."

She chuckled. "Somehow I thought you did."

"So what happened next?"

"The party had lots of music and singers and dancers. Everyone was having a wonderful time."

"Did the king make a friend?"

"Not at first. Among the group of singers and dancers he saw a beautiful goddess. The most beautiful goddess he had ever seen."

"Did he marry her?"

She stopped. In her mind the story stopped right there. Whose story was she telling and where had it come from? "I'm not sure. I don't know if she liked him."

"I hope they don't get married."

"Why do you say that?"

"My mum and dad are married and my dad is bad."

She hugged him tight. "Not all men are bad. I don't know why your dad does the things he does, but you must remember not all men are like that. What about Chris? He's nice, isn't he?"

Jack smiled tentatively. "I guess so."

"And you're a boy, and one day you'll grow up to be a man."

He shook his head back and forth. "Nuh-uh. Not going to be a man."

"It's okay. You'll be a wonderful man one day. Your mummy will teach you how."

"Nope. I don't wanna be a man and do bad things."

Her heart broke for him. She tried desperately to keep the tears at bay. She turned him to face her directly. "Look into my eyes, Jack."

His eyes widened as he made an extra effort to stare at her.

"Good. Now let me tell you, there is no way you will be a bad man unless you want it to happen. You won't do bad things because you know they are bad."

"Yeah?"

"Yeah. I promise."

He threw his arms around her neck and hugged her tightly. "I love you, Callie!"

Her throat tightened as she gently rubbed her hand back and forth over his small head. His hair smelled like fruit and innocence, but if his father had his way, the innocence would be stolen from him way before his time. "I love you too, Jack."

He shifted on her lap and let go of her neck. She thought she heard a sound coming from upstairs so she lifted him off and sat him down on the couch before standing up. "You stay here and wait for me. I need to go upstairs for a minute."

He'd already moved forward and was playing with a puzzle on the coffee table. Her heart pounded as another noise sounded from overhead. She took the steps one at a time, keeping her movements silent. She stopped at the landing and waited, listening for more activity. Hearing nothing more, she kept going until she reached the top.

She took her mobile phone out of her pocket and keyed in the emergency number and kept her finger poised above the call button while she walked silently along the upstairs hall in search of the room the muffled noise had come from.

Damn! The door was closed. She leaned on the surface with her ear, listening for anything that might tell her what was happening. When she heard nothing, she twisted the handle slowly before opening the door a few inches.

A breeze swept through the window and she saw the curtain bumping against the railing. She let out a sigh of relief as she crossed the room and closed the window before clearing the phone and putting it back in her pocket. She'd just started back down the stairs when she heard the door's squeaky hinges move. She stopped and turned to see a masked man walking down the hall in her direction.

Oh no!

She ran down the stairs to the lounge room, took Jack by the hand and headed to the front door. "We have to leave, sweetie," she whispered. "Now."

"Why? I wanna 'nother story."

She tugged on his hand and picked him up, opting to carry him instead. "Can't tell you why now. We just have to get out."

"No one is leaving," said the masked man as he stood in front of the door, blocking her path.

Jack clutched Callie's shoulders and pulled himself closer to her. "It's my daddy," he whispered.

Callie fought back a scream and ran with Jack in the other direction toward the back door. "I know, but don't worry, sweetie. I'll look after you."

As she struggled one-handed with the bolt and the lock, the intruder caught up with them.

"You can't escape me so give up."

She reached into her pocket for her phone, but he lifted the gun and pointed it at her and Jack.

"Put the phone down on the floor."

"I won't call anyone, I promise."

"What do you think I am, an idiot? Throw. The. Phone. Down."

She complied, flinging it across the room as far away from him as she could.

"Good. Now tell me where Sarah is."

Oh, god! No wonder she ran away from her husband.

"She's not here."

He grunted. "I can see that. Tell me where she is, and no one will get hurt."

Callie gripped Jack tighter to her body and whispered in his ear, "Don't say anything Jack." The brave little boy trembled but said nothing.

"I don't know where she is."

He waved the gun in front of their faces. "I don't believe you. Tell me now, or I'll take the boy."

Jack clung to her and burrowed his head into her neck.

"There's no need for that. I really don't know where she is."

Jack turned his head and shouted at the man. "Don't you hurt my mummy!"

The man leaned forward and slapped Jack on the back. "Shut up, kid. I won't hurt anyone if you tell me where she is."

Jack burrowed even closer and cried against her neck. "No!"

Jack's father moved forward and Callie slipped away to the side but not in time to prevent him from grabbing hold of Jack's arm.

"Come on, you little shit. Tell me where your mother is or I'll beat the crap out of you."

Callie hugged Jack close to her body. "Don't hurt him," she cried. "He's only a baby, and he's your son!"

He swiped the mask off his head and threw it aside. "You like him?" he taunted. "You can keep him. I only want his mother." He took a step closer and wrenched Jack's arm again. "Tell me where she is!"

Jack winced but he didn't cry. His grip on her neck tightened and he stayed firmly in her arms. "I hate you!" he shouted.

His father raised his hand, but Callie was faster, kicking his knee out from under him before she took off running toward the hallway.

He grunted loudly as he fell back onto the floor. "Come back here you bitch! I haven't finished with you yet."

Her heart pounded as she made her way to the front door. With only one hand, the task of opening all three locks proved impossible, Footsteps thudded on the ground, increasing her panic. Her hands trembled and her heart sank

* * * *

Gus paced up and down the footpath across the road from Serenity. It was a fitting name for a place where people sought peace. His heart ached as he thought about the reasons why his Calliope was drawn to that place. He knew Pandora was trouble, but it never occurred to him that her meddling would be so successful. If he was lucky enough to win her back and she returned home with him, he would make certain she never had cause to doubt his loyalty again. He would prove his love to her with every day and she would never feel insecure again. She meant so much to him and she deserved to feel cherished.

He caught a sound coming from across the street and stopped walking so he could hear what it was.

What in Hades? He raced toward the noise, convinced it was a cry of pain. He rushed toward the door and was joined by one of the men helping to watch the house.

"Who are you?" the policeman yelled, pushing in front of him to prevent him from opening the door.

"There's no time for that," said Gus. "Did you hear that cry?"

He shook his head. "I don't know what you're talking about. What cry?"

Gus stepped forward and tried the front door handle. "I heard someone cry out from inside this house."

"Step away from the door." The man pulled out a mobile phone and started tapping on the screen.

Gus ignored him, turning the handle again only to find it wouldn't budge. "It is locked. Do you have a key?"

He held up his hand and started talking into his phone. "Chris. It's Mick. You might want to come down here, there's a strange guy hanging around claiming he heard someone cry out from inside the house." He nodded as he listened to the reply. "Uh-huh. Yep. No, not him, it's someone else. That's what I thought. No worries. I'll see you soon."

Gus investigated the door, discovering a number of locks holding the door in place. Closing his eyes, he concentrated on the door and gently pushed. The door swung open into the empty hallway and he walked inside.

"Hey," the man called behind him. "You can't go in there. I'm a cop and I'll arrest you if I have to."

Gus wasn't waiting for anyone. Not when his wife was in danger. "Stop wasting time. We need to find everyone, and see if they are safe."

The policeman Gus now knew as Mick, pulled a gun out of a holster under his coat and pushed past Gus, heading in the direction of the front room. "Stay here while I take a look around."

Gus followed him. As a king in his homeland, Gus did not take orders from others very well. "I do not think so. We will accomplish more if we work together, and I am far from helpless."

Mick shrugged. "Suit yourself. It's your funeral. But stay close. I don't want to have to go look for you as well."

Gus nodded as he scanned the empty room. It was very neat and obviously used for entertainment with a couple of large comfortable chairs and a low table scattered with books and children's toys. He continued through to the adjoining room to find the kitchen in disarray. The door leading to the back yard was wide open, and just inside was an upturned chair blocking the exit.

Mick followed him, stopping in the entrance. "Shit. This doesn't look good. You check the other rooms down here and I'll look upstairs."

"It is too late. There is no one here."

"I think you may be right, mate, but it's my job to make sure. My partner will be here any second now, so hang tight."

Gus gripped his hands into fists, tapping them against his thighs to prevent him from hitting something. He had led his soldiers and fought in many battles, but he had never felt fear like he did at this moment. He prayed to the gods Calliope would be safe. He closed his eyes and checked the remainder of the rooms, sensing for Calliope and her friends, but he already knew he would find no one.

Where are you, Calliope?

He heard a commotion out the front before a man he recognized as one he had seen with Calliope and her friends came running into the room.

"What the fuck happened here—and where's Mardi?" His eyes narrowed in Gus' direction. "And who the fuck are you?"

"I am Gus, husband of Calliope," he said. "And it looks like someone has taken her and the others away."

"Husband? Shit. I'm a cop. My name's Chris and I am also Mardi's boyfriend. Where is everyone then?"

"I do not know where they are, but it is apparent there was trouble here."

"That's a bloody understatement," he said.

The other cop returned to the room at that moment and they both put their guns back into their holsters. If this was the extent of law enforcement in this land, Gus was worried for their chances of finding everyone before they got hurt. Although he recognized the dangers of using magic too overtly in a society that had little belief, as soon as he could manage it, he would be consulting with Eros to find Calliope's exact position.

Chris walked over to the kitchen bench and slammed his fist on the counter. "What the fuck happened, Mick? You were supposed to be watching them."

"I know, mate. I'm sorry. I didn't take my eyes of the house, but whoever it was must have snuck in via the back lane."

"Wasn't Jackson meant to be covering the back?"

"Yeah, but he had to go and start his shift. Mackenzie should be arriving any time now. There was probably a window of five or ten minutes with no one there."

"Bastard. Jeezus, he must have known our schedule." Chris leaned forward and smelled a substance on the counter top. He pulled a pair of latex gloves out of his pocket and donned the before rubbing the red liquid through his fingertips. "Shit. This is blood."

Gus' whole body went cold. He headed toward the open door so he could summon Eros, but instead ran into Mardi and another woman.

Chris ran across the room and threw his arms around Callie's friend, squeezing her tight and lifting her off the floor. "Mardi! Thank god you're all right!"

She laughed. "Of course I'm all right. It was Sarah who cut her hand." She looked from Chris to Mick to Gus then back to Chris. "Hang on a minute. What's going on? Where are Callie and Jack?"

Sarah screamed, her hands covering her face. "Oh, my God. Oh, my God! It's Adam, isn't it? He's got them."

Chapter Six

Callie walked around the room, checking for anything that might help them get away. Adam, Sarah's husband, had driven them out of the city and locked them in an old shed on a remote property. They'd had no chance to escape so far as Adam kept his weapon trained on Jack at all times. She'd promised Jack she'd look after him so she'd followed Adam's instructions under sufferance.

She had no idea where they were, since her and Jack had been tied together on the floor of a van and a blanket had been thrown over them, but she knew it wasn't suburban on account of the large and open land that surrounded the shed and the immense quiet. Not a sound of a car was evident. She heard only the whisper of wind through the trees outside and the occasional cacophony of the kookaburras laughing in the distance.

Callie estimated they'd been there for at least an hour, but she was already going stir crazy. Confined spaces were apparently not her thing. Jack, the little trooper, was being so brave, huddled quietly on a pile of hessian rugs in the corner. Callie had waited until they'd heard the van drive away before she'd started her search and she didn't have very long. Adam had promised them he would be back soon, and he wanted answers. The man was definitely unhinged. He couldn't possibly think he would get away with this, even if he did find Sarah. There was only so much he could expect his former cop friends to turn a blind eye to. Kidnapping would certainly push over those boundaries. That's what worried her the most. If he knew he was going to be caught, he had nothing to lose and that meant she and Jack were in terrible danger. She had to find a way to get them out of there as soon as possible.

She took in a breath and exhaled slowly while she examined the frame of the window again. She pushed it with both hands, but it was a lot sturdier than it looked and didn't budge. No luck with the door either. She wiped her dust-covered hands on the legs of her jeans and stood back, praying that another plan would come to her. There had to be a way out of here…time was running out.

Something tugged at her jeans and she turned to find Jack peering at her. "Callie, I'm scared."

"I'm scared too, Jack." She leaned over and picked him up. "But we will get out of here." She brushed hair off his face and planted a light kiss on his forehead. "I promise you I'll keep you safe."

Jack nodded, his lips quivering. He tried and failed to stop the sobs from breaking out and her heart broke. She rested her chin on his head and gently rocked him, whispering soft words she hoped would reassure him. She stood still and scanned the remaining walls, looking for any sign of a defect she could utilize as an escape route, but she wasn't having any luck.

Jack's trembling stopped and his breathing settled down into an even pattern. He'd fallen asleep, the poor little mite. She gently laid him down on the makeshift hessian bed and stood up, stretching her arms above her head and lengthening her spine. After being confined for so long, her body ached from head to toe, but she had to get back to work. It was times like these she wished she really *was* the goddess Gus believed her to be. A few magical powers would certainly come in handy right about now. When he'd kissed her, that floating thing had been quite convincing, but she was sure it was some type of trick. If she had powers, she'd certainly know it, wouldn't she?

She was interrupted by the sound of tires crunching on gravel and she pulled back from the door. *Darn the gods.*

Jack woke up and ran to her as the door opened and their captor came back into the shed.

Callie placed her hand on Jack's shoulder to steady him while she stood her ground. "We've already told you we don't know where Sarah is, so keeping us here is not going to help you find her."

He laughed. His hair fell across his eyes, hiding half his face. "I've given up on getting your co-operation. I've got a much better idea."

Callie's stomach clenched and her skin went cold. "What do you mean?"

He shook his head, his unkempt hair uncovering his face, revealing the bloodshot eyes of a man who drank too much and slept too little. "Don't you worry about it, bitch. Just keep the kid quiet and everything will be fine."

"Please. You can't leave us here. We won't tell anyone if you will just let us go."

"Sure you won't," he chuckled. He turned to leave and threw a brown paper bag and a couple of water bottles on the floor. "Here's your dinner. The kid knows I always bring him a treat. You can see, I'm not mistreating you, so just do what I say and no one gets hurt."

Callie waited until he'd closed the door before picking up the bag. The unmistakable aroma of burgers and fries sent her stomach into overdrive.

Jack's stomach growled in unison with hers but he waited for a signal from her. "Can we have some?"

"Hang on a minute while I check it's not spoiled," she said, opening the bag and taking out a burger wrapped in paper. She set the bag down then unwrapped the burger, turning it over, separating the buns and smelled inside. Satisfied, she put it back together and handed it to Jack. "It seems okay but don't eat it too quickly. We don't know how long it will be before we get any more food."

* * * *

Gus wanted to hit something. Hard. But he restrained himself, fearful of what damage he could do in this mortal world. What in Hades was taking Eros so long?

He walked back inside the house. Perhaps the law enforcers would have some new information by now, although he doubted it, given their incompetence in keeping his Calliope safe so far.

Calliope's friend Mardi stood up from sitting on the couch and comforting Sarah. From what he had gleaned, her name was Sarah, and it was her husband who had abducted Calliope and his son. What kind of man did that to his own family? He'd seen it happen in his own kingdom, and it always sickened him. A man should cherish and protect his family, not cause them pain. Men such as this monster deserved the most painful of punishments.

Mardi turned at his approach. "Hey, you! Gus. Aren't you supposed to have special powers?"

Her boyfriend, Chris, stared at them both and narrowed his gaze before continuing his conversation with his partner.

Oeagus lowered his voice. "Calliope told you about me?"

She smiled. "Of course she did. We're best friends. We tell each other everything. So can't you just wave a hand and bring them both back here?"

"If it were that simple, don't you think I would have done it already?"

She frowned. "So you lied to her. You're not all powerful."

He shrugged. "I did not lie, but my powers are limited in this world. I must know the location so I can see Calliope and the child in my mind before I can help them."

"So we're screwed then."

"Perhaps your police friends will have some suggestions."

"I'm not holding my breath. Sarah's husband used to be one of them, so he knows how to hide and not be found. Can't you do anything?"

"So now you believe I am who I say I am?"

"At this point I'm willing to try anything," said Mardi.

Gus spied movement outside the window. He followed it with his eyes and headed toward the door.

Mardi caught up, peering to the side of him. "What is it?"

"Help may have just arrived."

"Who is it?"

"A friend. You must trust me and do not repeat what you see or hear, no matter how strange it may appear."

"Don't worry. No one would believe me anyway. If it helps us find Callie and Jack, I'd run naked through the streets."

"I do not think that will be necessary," he said solemnly.

"I was only joking."

He nodded. "I understand. A small levity to relieve the stress."

Mardi laughed. "Um. Yeah. That's it."

"Do not leave here, I will return."

"We're not going anywhere," she said as he walked out of the door.

Gus found Eros chatting to a female police officer in the lane behind the house. "What took you so long?"

Eros smiled at the woman breaking away to join Gus. "I'm sorry, but I was attending to my many charges. I cannot drop everything and come each time you call."

"This is urgent. Calliope has been abducted."

He stopped smiling immediately. "What?"

"Yes, while you have been cavorting with your lovers, my beloved has been taken prisoner by a madman."

"I was not cavorting. I help people connect, but that's neither here nor there. A hundred apologies, my friend. I did not know."

Gus shrugged. "You are here now and I have need of your help."

"Of course. Anything you need. What do you wish me to do?"

"Can you find them?"

"Them? I thought you were speaking of Calliope."

"There are two to rescue. This madman has also taken a child."

Eros frowned. "The monster! I'll try to find their location and report back to you. You know I am unable to use violence, but if I have an opportunity I can help them to escape. In this world my powers are limited to matters of the heart."

"Yes, I am aware, and mine are limited. It seems I can only transport to places I can visualize."

"One of the limitations of the mortal world, but useful so that we do not cause chaos."

"I understand the reasoning, but that is not helping us right now."

"Yes, of course. I will be on my way so that I may find Calliope and the child. I will report as soon as I have located them. Hopefully they are still being held together."

"My Calliope has a protective streak many miles long. I have no doubt she will keep him safe with her at all costs."

"Maybe she will regain her memory and defeat the man?"

"I wish that were true, but surely she would have already returned if that were the case?"

Eros nodded. "Of course." He turned to leave. "I'll be back soon with news."

"Thank you, my friend. May the speed of the gods be with you."

Gus watched his friend vanish and sighed. Hopefully Eros would have a location soon. His stomach clenched while he imagined all the worst-case scenarios Calliope could be experiencing at this very minute. The most frustrating thing was that he had no knowledge of this enemy, so he had no idea how best to fight him.

He twisted back toward the house and Mardi met him at the door.

"Did that guy just vanish into thin air?"

He placed his finger over his lips. "You promised not to speak of what you see."

"Sheesh. You mean I did actually see that?"

"Yes. Eros did disappear. He has gone to see if he can find Calliope."

"Cool. Let's hope he can find them...wait, did you say his name was Eros?"

"I did."

"Oh, my God. Eros. Isn't he the God of Love?"

"He likes to think so."

"I thought all of that stuff was myth."

"Most myths start based on truth. Why would this be any different?"

She shook her head. "Holy shit. Greek mythology is true. Who would have thought?"

"Not all of us are from Greece. I am from Thrace, although we are ruled by Zeus."

Mardi walked out into the yard. "So this means I'll be losing Callie if we get her back safely."

"I will rescue her, but it will be her decision to come back with me or stay here. She makes her own destiny."

"Wow. You really do know her."

"Of course. I am her husband. Calliope needs to find her own way. I cannot tell her what to do or it will stifle her."

"Do you have a brother? I have a sister who's single."

"No, I do not. Why do you ask?"

"Never mind. What happens now? When will your friend return?"

"I do not know, but hopefully soon so I can rescue them before that madman harms them."

"God, I hope so too."

Chris walked outside to join them, his face grim.

"What news have you of Calliope and the boy?" asked Gus.

"Nothing good. No one has any idea where he might be hiding out and there were no clues when his house was searched. There's also no record of any property he either rents or owns."

"In other words you've got zip," said Mardi.

"That's about it," he said. "But I'm going to question Sarah again in case she can think of anything that might help us."

"Go easy on her," said Mardi.

"I know what I'm doing, Mardi."

She wrapped her arms around his waist and laid her head against his chest. "I know, sweetie. I'm just worried about her."

Chris cradled her head in his hand and kissed her forehead. "We'll find them. I promise."

Gus watched the couple, remembering another time when he and Calliope had shared such moments. When he found his wife he would convince her their love was worth fighting for, but if Eros did not hurry it might be too late.

* * * *

Callie grimaced as another nail broke. Since Jack had fallen asleep some time ago, she'd been scratching at the door trim to see if there was any way she could loosen it. She made another attempt to work the old wood away from the lock, but the pain in her fingers was too much. She sucked the end of her fingertips to soothe the burning and tried to think of another plan, but she was all out of ideas. She prayed to the gods that someone would work out where they were being kept prisoner, and soon. Preferably before that crazy man returned. The only thing they had on their side was that despite his threats, he was yet to harm them. Added to that was the fact that he'd fed them, which could mean he most likely planned to keep them alive, at least for now. It wasn't much, but it gave her hope that Gus or the police would find them in time.

Jack sighed in his sleep and turned over, his hand resting under his cheek. It was incredible that he could look so peaceful when they were under so much stress. Callie tucked a strand of his hair that had fallen over his eyes behind his ear. He was such a brave kid. He'd seen more violence in the short time he had been on Earth than any person should see in a lifetime, but he was still a sweet and innocent child. Sarah was doing a wonderful job with him. Callie's womb clenched at the possibility of one day having her own little boy. Pictures of a cute baby with blond curls and brilliant blue eyes had her smiling, but she shook her head to shrug off the image. Now was not the time. They had to get out of here, not spend time mooning about the man who claimed to be her husband.

But maybe that was the way she should go? He not only claimed to be her husband, but also that she was a goddess and he a god. That trick in the coffee shop had been pretty convincing. Maybe she could contact him? She closed her eyes and brought up an image of him in her mind.

Gus.

She paused to listen but heard nothing.

Gus.

She called his name louder inside her head.

"Can you hear me, Gus?"

A distinctive voice spoke inside her head, *"Calliope?"*

She jumped up and down on the spot. *Holy goddess, it worked!*

The voice returned. *"Calliope – where are you? We are searching for you. Did Eros find you?"*

"Eros? The guy who's supposed to be my cousin? Never mind. No, to answer your question. No one has found us. Can you get us out of here?"

"I need to see where you are. Can you show me?"

"Show you? I have no idea where we are. How can I show you?"

"Use your eyes, my love. Look around where you are and show me in your mind."

A car drove up outside and cut its engine.

"I can't do it right now, we have company."

"Calliope! Show me so I can come and rescue you!"

The door slammed open and Adam stormed into the room.

She stared at him, hoping the scene would somehow get through to Gus so he might find a way to get there.

"Can you see him?"

"Yes, but I need to see landmarks. Can you go outside?"

"I'll try, but he doesn't look happy so I don't like my chances."

"Stay safe, my love. Do not take risks."

Adam rushed towards her. "Who the fuck are you talking to?"

Oh no. He heard me. "I'm speaking to the gods."

He laughed at her. "Ha. Fat lot of good that will do you."

"I'm praying that you'll let us go."

Adam snorted. "As I said, fat lot of good that will do."

"What do you plan to do with us?"

"You're going get me my wife back."

"How do you plan to do that when no one knows where we are?"

"Good point. We might have to do something about that."

"I'm waiting with baited breath."

He slapped her across the cheek, sending her falling to the ground. "Shut your face, bitch!"

Her jaw ached. She rubbed her hand over her face to ease the pain.

"Calliope? Did he strike you?"

She stood up, determined not to show him how rattled she was.

"I'm fine."

"If you can't show me where you are, tell me about this place. Perhaps Chris and the police can find it if they have more details."

"Praying again?"

"Can't talk now. Busy." She severed the connection because now anger replaced her fear. She remembered what he had done to Sarah and Jack, and how fear had not helped them at all. How dare he treat women that way!

"No. I'm thinking of ways I can make you pay."

He took a step closer to her, his fist clenched and his face thunderous. "You have a mouth on you, bitch. Keep that up and you'll see what I do to women who give me lip."

"Oh, I've seen what you do. You cowards are all the same. You pick on people you think are weaker than you, but when they challenge you, you don't know what to do, so you hit them. So clever. *Not.*"

She stepped back when he leaned closer to her.

"Shut your mouth, you bitch, or I'll…"

"You'll do what?" she said. She edged her way along the wall toward the door.

He lunged at her but she side-stepped, inching even closer to escape.

Jack woke up and started crying, distracting Adam. "Shut up, kid."

"Lovely the way you speak to your son. Such a great role model."

He screwed up his features and his face went red. She was pretty certain she saw steam coming out of his ears. He lifted his clenched fist and took a swipe in her direction, but she was too quick for him, ducking and diving out of the door.

"Come back here, woman!"

She turned around and spied young Jack standing at the door, staring at her as Adam chased after her.

"Run, Jack! Run and hide!"

Her chest hurt but she kept running. She passed Adam's car and sped up the driveway, hoping to come to a road as soon as possible. *Please get away, Jack!*

She attempted to project what she was seeing around her inside her head. *"Gus? Can you see this?"*

"Yes, my love, but I cannot see clearly. When it is safe, can you stop for a short time?"

She snuck a peek behind her and saw Adam gaining on her. *"Not at the moment."*

Up ahead she spied a letterbox at the top of the steep driveway. *"I'm going to try something so don't go away."*

"I will stay with you as long as it takes, Calliope."

She hoped he meant it because she didn't have time to chat. She dug deep and increased her speed, hoping to reach her target before Adam caught up with her.

She prayed Jack had managed to find a good hiding place since this running gig was no fun, and she didn't want it to be all for nothing.

When she was almost to the top of the hill, two things happened. Her shins burned, sending shards of pain through her legs, and she finally eyeballed the letterbox. She sighed when she read the lettering. 'The Willows' was all it said. No number. No street name. Nothing. *Damn the gods!*

She leaned over the wooden box to peer inside, but it was empty.

Adam grabbed her wrist and yanked her toward him, spinning her around. Before she could take a breath, he tied both her hands together with plastic cord.

"You expecting mail?"

Her throat constricted and her eyes watered, but she sucked in a breath. She wouldn't cry. She never cried. "You never know who's going to send you something unexpectedly."

"*Calliope? We will find you. Stay strong.*"

"*Hurry.*"

"*We will try, my love.*"

Adam tugged at her and dragged her back down the driveway toward the shed. "Are you praying again?"

She chose not to answer him. He tugged on her arms, and they burned painfully. He pulled her along with him, not caring if she could keep up or not. If the gods were smiling on her then Gus had gotten enough to figure out where they were because she was running out of ideas.

Adam threw her on the ground inside the shed and slammed the door shut. He slid the lock in place and she smiled when she realized Jack had gotten away. At least something was accomplished.

"Don't get too comfortable, bitch," he shouted through the door. "After that stunt you pulled I'm going to have to change my plans and you're gonna have to pay for that. I'll be back to show you what I do to bad girls who don't follow my orders."

She shivered. She remembered the pictures of the many battered women she'd seen in the shelter. If she'd read him right, Adam was going to do a lot worse to her.

"Hurry, Gus."

She sat on the pile of rags and waited for him to answer her. When he didn't she hoped it meant he was on his way there. She lay down and rolled on her side and waited for whatever came next.

* * * *

Gus walked over to the kitchen table and sat next to Sarah. "What do you know of a place called 'The Willows'?"

She jumped, visibly shaken. "How do you know about The Willows?"

His heart leaped. "So you know where this place is?"

"Yes, I had forgotten about it, but how did you know?"

"That's not important. I believe your husband has taken the child and Calliope there. Can you give us directions?"

"Of course."

He smiled for the first time in hours. "Excellent. Let's go and tell Chris."

In less than ten minutes he joined Chris and his partner, Mick, in the police car as they sped toward the farm where his beloved was being held. Chris turned around from the front seat and leaned forward.

"Look, mate. I don't know how you came by this information, but it seems like it could be a winner. That doesn't mean you can go off half-cocked. I want you to stay in the car when we get there. This bloke is dangerous."

"If by 'half-cocked' you mean running into the house unprepared, then I can assure you I have no intention of doing that. In my country I am considered one of the best battle tacticians there are. We must find the lie of the land first, then formulate a plan of attack."

"Exactly...no, I mean—that's my job. You need to stay out of the way. I shouldn't even be bringing you with us."

"I can be of great use to you, and I am most grateful to be here."

"I'd be out of a job if I let a civilian get involved in an incident so spare me your gratitude, mate, because you're gonna have to stay in the car."

He nodded and sat against the seat in the rear. "Fine." What Chris didn't know was that as soon as they figured out where Calliope and the child were being held he would flash in, grab them and flash out. Having the car close would be useful.

Mick increased the speed of the police car as Chris tapped into a screen he called GPS, which apparently would help them find where they were going.

"How long until we arrive?"

Chris glanced at the screen. "Another five minutes."

"Are there others joining us?"

"Yeah. Area Command has sent three other cars but we're going to stay back a bit until we get a copy of the floor plan of the property. Then we'll have a better idea of the best strategy."

"Is there any way to get there faster?"

"I'm driving as fast as I can, mate."

"Aren't police allowed to drive faster in the course of their work?"

"Sure, but that requires the siren. We don't want to alert Adam that we're there."

How could he tell them that it didn't matter? He could deal with this maniac with a snap of his fingers, but he needed to avoid that line of thought. Eros had warned him not to show off his magic. These mortals tended to get overexcited about it, and the last thing he needed was to draw too much attention to himself. He would have to wait for an opportunity, but if it didn't come easily, he would get them out any way he could.

The car pulled off the highway and headed a short way down a narrow road. A few minutes later they reached the other police cars, which were parked at a truck stop. A number of policemen in uniforms stood around a picnic table as one of them pointed to a map that was spread out over the surface.

Chris turned to Gus. "Remember what I said. You need to stay in the car."

"I will do anything that will help Calliope and the boy."

Chris gave him a pointed look. "I mean it."

"I promise I will not do anything to endanger anyone."

Chris got out of the front seat and leaned in to the car. "Glad to hear it."

"Are you coming, Mick?"

Mick opened his door and climbed out. "Hold your horses."

Gus watched them walk over to the other policeman, wishing he could hear what they were saying. He hated waiting, but given that this enemy was in a land he knew nothing about, he depended on the soldiers of the police to use their knowledge of this evil. Gus was not familiar with the weapons of this land either, so for the time being he needed to stay put.

A number of the police headed off toward the area that he believed Callie to be so he spent the time waiting and praying to the gods that he would have his Calliope back soon.

One of the cops returned, carrying what looked like a hat of some sort. He showed Chris who took put on some gloves before taking it from him and examining it closely. He placed it in a plastic bag and brought it over to the car, bending down to speak to Gus through the open window. "They've found a hat belonging to Adam, so we've confirmed that they were here at least. Let's hope they still are."

Gus leaned forward on the seat. "You think that they might not be?"

"You never know, he might have moved them somewhere else. He has to know it's only a matter of time until we find this place."

His heart stopped. He did not wish to think about not finding them right now. "They must be here."

"Don't worry mate. We'll find them."

"I trust you are right."

"So do I," he said as he walked back to the others. "So do I."

"She is near, my friend. I can sense her."

Gus jumped. "Damn the Gods, Eros—you should warn me before you appear like that."

"Don't tell me the humans are making you soft?"

"It is my fear for Calliope that has me on edge. Quickly—tell me what you have learned."

"Of course. As I said, I can feel her. She is very near."

"Take me to her."

"As you wish," he said, grasping Gus by the wrist and flashing them away.

They re-appeared behind group of police carrying guns as they approached an old shed. Chris was holding some sort of device up to his mouth and shouting through it.

"Come out Simpson! We have the farm surrounded. There is no escape."

Adam appeared at the door, the weapon in his hands held high and aimed at the tactical response officer closest to the shed. "Stand back or the boy and the woman die."

Jack chose that moment to run out of the bushes toward Chris.

Chris snatched him up into his arms and handed him to the cop beside him who took him back toward the car. "We have the boy Simpson. Now let the woman go."

Adam swore. "You little piece of shit. I don't care about the boy, but I'm not letting the woman go until I have my wife back."

Gus moved forward, but Eros gripped his shoulder, holding him back.

"Leave him to the police. We can save Calliope."

Gus nodded. "All right. Come with me, but I will punish him for what he has done."

"No problem. Let's get them out of there."

Gus closed his eyes and transported into the shed to find Callie huddled in the corner. Relieved that she appeared unharmed, he ran toward her.

Calliope's eyes grew wide. "Gus—look out!"

A shot ran out as Gus turned around.

Adam shifted and lunged at him, rifle in hand. "Where the fuck did you come from?"

Gus grabbed for the rifle, wresting it out of Adam's hand just as the gun discharged.

Adam came at him, punching wildly. "I'll get my wife back and you can't stop me!"

Gus' blood raced through his body and his muscles expanded. "Eros, remove Calliope while I take care of this vermin."

"With pleasure," said Eros, taking Calliope by the hand before they disappeared from the room.

Adam spun, darting his eyes around. "Huh? Where did they go?"

Gus threw a punch directly to Adam's temple, sending him backwards to the floor. "Somewhere you will never find them."

"That's what you think, you bastard," yelled Adam. He pulled another gun from an ankle holster and fired.

The sound reverberated throughout the shed and Gus stopped as a sharp pain had him grabbing his side. He removed his hand to find it covered with the blood that trickled out of a hole in his shirt.

Chris and Mick stormed into the room to find him collapsed on the floor. The last thing he remembered before he lost consciousness was his beloved Callie wrapping her arms around him and begging him not to die. He fell asleep wondering why she thought he could die when he was an immortal?

Chapter Seven

Callie ran back into the shed. She saw her Oeagus lying on the ground, blood pouring out of his side and her heart stalled for a few beats. "Don't die on me, my beloved," she whispered to him as she cradled his head in her lap. "You can't die on me now. You may be an immortal, but you can still be killed."

He raised his head a few centimeters and his eyes flickered, but then he closed them again and he fell back against her thighs. She couldn't lose him now. She remembered him. She couldn't remember all of her life in Olympus, even her father and her sisters were all a blur, but the most important thing she remembered was her love for this gentle giant lying injured.

Paramedics arrived moments later, putting pressure on his wound and placing a needle in his hand to give him some fluids via a clear plastic bag.

Stop! She could heal him couldn't she?

Eros appeared at her side, his hand on her shoulder giving her much needed support. "If we spirit him away it will cause many questions, but I will do it if you wish, Calliope."

She nodded, understanding that her life here would be impossible if the mortals were to witness their powers. She spoke to the ambulance officers. "How badly is he injured?"

One of them smiled at her. "He's lost a lot of blood, but from what I can see it's not a deep wound so barring any infections, I'm expecting that he will make a full recovery. But we need to get him to hospital ASAP so the doctors can stop the bleeding."

She made a quick decision and prayed to the gods it was the right one. "May I travel with him in the ambulance? I am his wife."

Eros smiled and stepped back into the shadows.

The paramedic, who was attaching a plastic collar to Gus' neck, nodded. "No worries, love, but you'll need to stay back and leave us to do our job."

"Of course," she said, standing back to allow the paramedics to raise the gurney to wheel it to the ambulance.

Mardi and Sarah arrived with Jack firmly gripping his mother around the neck. Mardi took her by hand and tucked Callie's arm under her own. "Thank goodness you're okay.

"How did you get here?" asked Callie.

Mardi squeezed her hand. "I drove us up here. Don't worry—we waited with the police until it was clear to come in."

"Thanks for bringing Sarah up for Jack. He's been through a lot."

"Yes, the poor little guy, but what about you? You've been through the mill too."

"I'll be fine, but it's Gus I'm worried about."

"Is he going to be okay?"

"He'd better. We have some time to catch up on."

Mardi gasped. "So you remember him now huh?"

Callie gave her a small smile. "I remember some of it. I will tell you more after I know he will recover."

The paramedic pointed to the back of the ambulance. "You coming?"

"Absolutely." She turned to Mardi and touched her hand. "Make sure Jack is okay. I'll call you later."

"No way. I'm not leaving you. I'll meet you at the hospital and keep you company."

Her eyes filled with tears as she climbed in next to Gus. "Thanks. I'll see you soon."

The drive to the hospital was endless. Gus remained unconscious while the paramedic continued to monitor his vital signs. It was difficult to even see his face with the oxygen mask covering his mouth and nose but the only positive was that the bleeding seemed to have slowed down. The dressing was reinforced with tape and no further seepage could be seen. *Thank the gods for small mercies.*

As she sat, memories of the many years of their time together flooded back. How could she not have recognized this wonderful man? He was, and always would be, her soul mate, and her heart ached at the pain she must have caused him. She still had no idea why and how she had arrived here in the mortals' land, but that wasn't important right now. Her main worry was to get Gus well again so they could be together.

The ambulance pulled up at the emergency department and the doors flew open. The paramedics pulled the gurney out of the van and wheeled Gus inside.

"What do you have for us?" asked a man in green scrubs with the title 'Doctor' embroidered across his pocket.

"Gunshot to the lower right quadrant. Doesn't appear to be very deep, and the bleeding seems to have slowed down. BP is ninety over fifty and pulse one hundred and twenty. His resps are shallow but slow at fourteen. Not sure what that's about, but at least his oxygen sats are ninety-nine percent on ten liters via the non-rebreather mask."

The paramedics wheeled him into a cubicle and pulled the curtains.

A nurse in blue scrubs stopped Callie from entering. "Sorry, but you can't go in there right now."

"But he's my husband," she pleaded, her heart thumping.

The nurse gestured to a seat across the other side of the room. "I understand, and you can go in soon, but the doctors and nurses need to assess him first. We'll let you know what's going on as soon as we do, I promise."

She shuffled to the other side of the corridor and sat down. "Thank you.

The nurse gave her a slight smile. "It's my job. Can I get you a cup of tea?"

"No, that's very kind of you, but I don't think I could handle anything in my stomach right now."

The nurse frowned as she inspected Callie's bruised and bleeding hands. "You're hurt too. Come with me and we'll fix you up."

"No. I can't leave Gus."

"You won't be much use to him like this. It won't take long."

"Can't you do it here? I'd rather be here when Gus wakes up."

The nurse looked around. "I'll see what I can do."

Callie let out a breath and relaxed. "That would be great. I really appreciate it."

The nurse grimaced. "You may change your mind when I get working on those hands of yours."

"Is she giving you trouble?"

Callie turned and saw Mardi rushing toward her. Her eyes filled with hot tears as she stood up and ran to her, wrapping her arms around her, her head against Mardi's shoulder. "Thanks for coming."

"As if I could stay away," she said, her arms tightening around Callie's shoulders. "But what's with the tears? Is Gus going to be okay?"

"The paramedics thought so, but I haven't heard anything yet."

The nurse backed away, heading inside the drawn curtains. "I'll see if there's any news, but when I get back we'll deal with your hands."

Callie's drew back and stared at her wounds, which were only now beginning to sting. "All right, but there's no hurry."

Mardi picked up her hand and gasped. "Oh, my God, what have you done to yourself?"

Callie snorted. "I must have scraped them when I was trying to find a way out of the shed that idiot had us locked in. Speaking of the bastard, what happened to him?"

"Chris arrested him. He'll be locked up for a long time. Sarah and Jack will be safe now."

"Thank the goddess for that. I can't believe evil like that exists here. He would have killed his own son."

Mardi took her by the arm and guided her to her seat, sitting beside her on the bench. "I've seen a lot of bad things in my time at Serenity. It's a mystery why people lose their humanity like that."

She thought of what she could remember of her own people back on Mount Olympus. "It's all about power. One person imposing their will onto another."

"Yes, that's definitely it. And if they can't get their own way, they destroy what they can't have for themselves."

"How do we stop them?"

"Now that's the sixty-four-thousand-dollar question. If I had the answer, I'd be a millionaire."

"In the meantime we continue to help these families find a safe place."

"That's exactly right." She smiled. "Does this mean you want to stay here even though you have your memory back?"

"It's not all back yet, so I can't be sure what the future holds, but yes, I do want to continue to help in any way I can. I'm not sure how much I will be able to do, but I promise I won't abandon you."

"I wouldn't blame you if you went back to your home with Gus."

She grasped her friend's hand. "I know you wouldn't, but what you do at Serenity is important, and it's come to mean a lot to me. I will be around to help—one way or another."

The nurse returned to let them know there was nothing yet to report, then proceeded to cleanse and dress Callie's hands. She finished wrapping the last finger in the plaster when the doctor came out from behind the curtains, his face grim.

"You're the patient's wife?"

She jumped out of the chair. "Yes. How is he?"

"He's stable for now. We've managed to close up the wound. It wasn't deep, but it's his conscious state that we're worried about. There doesn't seem to be a reason for him to be unconscious."

Mardi stood and joined her, holding on to her shoulder as Callie's world collapsed around her. "What does that mean? Is he going to be okay?"

The doctor shifted from one foot to another. "At this stage his vital signs are good. I've ordered an MRI of his head to see if we can find a reason for his coma. I'll have more news for you then."

"When will that be?"

"We've requested it urgently, but the procedure takes up to forty-five minutes, so it could be an hour or so before we know anything more. I suggest you go and have something to eat."

Callie dropped back down to the seat. "Thanks, Doctor. I don't think I can eat right now, so if you don't mind I'll stay here and wait for news."

"Suit yourself," he said.

Mardi sat next to her and patted her arm when the tall doctor left, but they both stood when the curtains opened again and Gus was wheeled out and pushed down the corridor toward the Radiology sign.

"Please stop for a second," she asked. "I want to see him."

"Sure, but not for long," the porter said.

"Thank you," she said as she leaned closely, examining his face. His pale skin matched the white sheets and his skin was cold and clammy. "I love you, Gus, my beloved. Come back to me," she whispered before kissing him lightly on the forehead. He had to get better. She was a goddess, so there must be something she could do, but at this moment she had no clue. She cursed the fates for her memories being taken from her. They were returning too slowly and she needed them right now.

"Sorry, dear, but we have to take him now."

She sat up, confused by her surroundings. "What? Oh, yes. Take care of him for me."

"I'll do that," the porter said. "We'll have him back in no time."

She kissed her hand and touched it to his head as the porter wheeled him away. She closed her eyes tightly, straining her mind for any memory at all of how she could help him, but nothing came to her.

"Don't force it, Calliope."

She swung around and collided with the firm body that was Eros. "Thank the goddess that you're here. I don't know how to help him. What should I do? Can we take him back to Mount Olympus?"

He smiled. "The answer is closer than you think. All that is required is for you to tap into that wellspring of love you have for each other."

"I've tried that already. It didn't work."

"You've tried it as a mortal. Not as a goddess. Try again."

"I'm not sure what you mean. I can't remember being a goddess, only that I am one and that Oeagus is my beloved."

He grinned at her. "That is all you need my dear cousin. When he returns, you will find a way to reach him and all will be well."

"But what if I can't do it?"

"We will worry about that when the time comes. Fear not, when it comes to love, I am always right."

"Always arrogant you mean."

He grinned. "That too. See, you are remembering."

She smiled. "Maybe I am."

"Hey, are you going to introduce me to this hunk of gorgeous man?"

"Mardi! Sorry…this is my cousin Erie."

Eros took Mardi's hand and bowed like the true gentleman he pretended to be. "Charmed to meet you, Mardi."

"Cousin? Wow — your relatives are multiplying. And what handsome men they are too."

"Careful. His head is big enough already. Plus his wife might not appreciate it."

Eros snorted. "I resent that. Pftt. My visage is revered in many kingdoms. And my wife understands the pressures of my job. She knows I love her above all others."

Mardi laughed. "I see what you mean, Callie. Maybe we should sic Jack on to him. A few hours with a four year old is always a good equalizer."

Eros' blue eyes crinkled at the corners. "Do your worst. Children also love me."

It was amazing how spending time with people she loved helped her cope with the gnawing pain of the fear she felt for Gus. However, it seemed like hours before Gus was wheeled back into his cubicle and the waiting was sending her crazy. When the doctor finally arrived he had nothing more to tell her. The MRI didn't show anything, which was good news, however it would be better to know what was going on. Gus remained unconscious, so she had to find the power within her to heal him and soon. Eros believed she could do it, so she would try, and she would succeed. She had to.

The kind nurse returned and showed her into the cubicle, finding a chair for her to sit on. She took hold of Gus' hand, his face peaceful and his breathing even. If she didn't know better she would think he was just sleeping, but the lack of animation in his features was so foreign to her memories that it hurt to watch him. She wrapped her other hand around his forearm to draw his hand closer and kissed his cool skin. Behind her closed eyes she searched for a memory or a feeling she could draw upon to bring her powers to the surface. She laid her head against his thigh and let a whirl of memories sweep through her. Wave after wave of scenes of their time together invaded her senses and sent tingles across all the nerve endings. She saw their wedding and the love that flowed between them. She saw them in their home in Thrace, and how Gus made her laugh. It wasn't all sweetness and light either, as she experienced some of their loud arguments, but making it up to each other was always intense, and afterwards their bond was stronger than ever.

The waterfall was one of her favorite places to go when she needed to think, but Oeagus was having none of that this time. She'd barely sunk into the cool waters of the pool that was fed from the underground springs when Gus wrapped his arms around her from behind and kissed her neck.

"Forgive me, my love," he whispered against her skin.

She turned toward him. "There is nothing to forgive. Just remember that I am a goddess and don't need you looking after me all the time."

"Let me look after you just this once."

She smiled. "No, it's my turn."

A spark of desire flared in his eyes as he disengaged from her touch and lay back in the pool, floating in the waist deep water. "Whatever you want, my beloved."

"You may regret saying that."

He winked as he remained there suspended just under the pool's surface, the water swirling patterns over the contours of his firm muscular body. "I could never regret time with you Calliope."

A wicked part of her personality took over as she ducked, completely submerging herself before rising out, her hands smoothing the fluid out of her eyes and her hair back. She let her head drop back, slightly pushing her breasts forward and thrusting her erect nipples close enough to Gus' face she could feel his hot breath brushing against her wet skin.

The sight of his thick erection making an appearance above the waterline urged her on to continue playing. She brought her hands to her breasts and she cupped them, then slowly worked her fingers toward her nipples, squeezing them gently at first, then increasing the tension on their sensitive tips. Despite the chill of the water, her body heat intensified when she looked down and caught Gus' gaze on her. He devoured her, but it was her face he was concentrating on, not her body. Never before had she seen such passion from just a look. It made her want more.

Slowly, she smoothed one hand across her belly and over her mound. She cupped her vulva and pushed gently with the heel of her hand. Sliding her index finger into the slit between her folds, she felt heat. When Oeagus was around, it didn't take much for her to be on fire.

Gus' voice rumbled deep in his throat. "Calliope…"

He was definitely forgetting his usual bossiness, so her plan must be working. She smiled to herself, feeling more confident by the second.

Step one down, time for step two.

Abruptly she removed her hands from her body and cupped some of the water, pouring it over her head and letting the cool fluid trickle over her face and breasts before slowly shaking her hair back and forth.

Oeagus groaned and his gorgeous cock rose even higher in the water.

She took a step closer to him, placing one hand on his forehead and another on his thigh. Their eyes met and stuck a light deep down in her soul. Her mouth went dry, and she licked her lips. She wanted to do this for him. It felt right and it felt good.

Smiling, she bent over and kissed him gently on the lips. "Your turn now."

She began a delicate trail with her fingers along his body, rubbing dirt off his muscles and dribbling water over his cuts. She reveled in his quick intake of breath as she moved down his abs and skimmed across the soft dusting of hair that led to his impressive erection.

"Be careful, Calliope, I'm going to either float upwards or sink to the bottom of the pool if you keep this up."

Moving past his erection and on to his thighs, she chuckled at the comical look of disappointment on his face.

"Just a few more minutes, lover boy."

She worked her fingers down to the end of his toes then stopped to kiss them one by one. Gus nearly sank there and then. If she hadn't steadied his hips, he would have.

"Turn over, Oeagus, I'm not finished relaxing you."

He laughed as he rolled over in the water. "I don't know how more relaxing I can take, my love."

Whack! *The muscles of his gorgeous arse contracted as she slapped her hand across both of his buns.*

"Ouch, what was that for?"

"To remind you who's in charge in our relationship."

He growled.

Loudly.

"I'll show you who's in charge!"

There was a large splash of water, and in the blink of an eye, she found herself being dragged out of the water and on her way back to the beach by the side of the pool.

"Don't drop me," she squealed, as she tugged against the firm grip he had around her wrist.

"When would I ever drop you, Calliope?" he shouted as he completed the short distance to the shore.

He set her down on the soft ground carefully but the gentleness was short-lived when he immediately pinned her down with his body covering hers and that enormous erection stabbing her belly. The look in his baby blue eyes was pure predator as he scooped up her wrists with one hand and drew her arms above her head.

Her whole body quivered in anticipation of what was to come. With her heart pounding and her breathing erratic, she waited for his next move.

His pupils dilated even further as his eyes met hers and fused with them. The hunger in his eyes was almost tangible. This was about raw sex. It was the burning flame between them, and it was possession. His possession of her body.

And she was more than willing to let him take what he wanted.

His eyes never left hers as his free hand began a slow trail of exploration starting from her hip and finishing at that sensitive area just below the curve of her breast. The soft touch of his long fingers sent shivers through her whole body. She sighed as her mouth opened and she arched her body, thrusting her breasts closer to him, begging him to touch them.

"You are mine, Calliope."

"Yes. Hurry up and prove it." *Her voice cracked as she spoke. She hardly recognized that low breathy and sexy sound coming from her own body. What was it about this man? He drove her crazy but he also knew all the right directions to push her.*

His deep, sexy laugh added another ten degrees to her body heat. *"You'll have to be patient, Calliope. All good things come to those who wait."*

"Well then, whatever the good thing is, get on with it!"

He leaned forward and blew on the buds of her nipples, making them pucker even more than before. He dipped his head again, this time to lave his tongue around a sensitive areole.

"Ahhhh," *she cried out.*

He nipped gently on the engorged tip, sending the equivalent of lightning bolts to her clit in a heady mixture of pleasure and pain. He kissed her breast, soothing the spot where his teeth had grazed. Their eyes met as his lips once again teased her skin, working their way up one kiss at a time toward her heated face. Letting go of her hands, he cupped her face, leaning all his weight onto his elbows. Those beautiful blue eyes darkened as his pupils dilated.

He didn't say a word.

He didn't have to.

Her breath caught as he moved in closer. His breath smelled of fruit, and that other ingredient that she knew to be his own unique taste.

His lips teased hers with a soft touch. His eyes closed as he came close again and covered her mouth with his while he teased and tantalized her. Moving with firm purpose, he sucked on her lower lip, scraping his teeth gently across her plump skin. His magic tongue slipped in as their breath mingled. He gently stroked her mouth, sending tingles straight through her chest to squeeze her heart. Moaning, she clamped her hands on his shoulders, itching to dig into his firm skin, but mindful of his injuries, she contented herself with just keeping a firm hold.

The kiss continued for what seemed like an eternity, but it would never be enough. When Oeagus drew back, they were both panting, desperate to draw in air before they began round two. He brought his head close again and kissed her once more on the lips then moved on to her neck, nuzzling in the hollow just above her shoulder. His hot breath tickled, setting off another set of shivers, and her body reacted by arching slightly. Her body burned for his touch.

"Gus, please touch me."

She could feel the smile against her skin as he continued to rub his nose against her neck.

"All in good time, woman. We can't rush things."

Oh God, if he didn't make a move soon, she would jump him, and that wouldn't be good for his bruises! "Fine," she said on a strangled sigh. "Just hurry!"

Just so he knew how serious she was, she arched her hips against him and slipped her legs around his thighs, trapping him against her dripping folds.

His cock heated and throbbed against her belly and Oeagus ground his hips even closer against her and growled in her ear.

"You don't play fair, my love."

She giggled as she lightly walked her fingers down his back to his firm buttocks and squeezed. "All's fair in love and war, Oeagus. Didn't anyone ever tell you that?"

"Oh yes," he said in that deep, raspy and sexy voice of aroused man that she loved to hear. "And here's another one for you. To the victor go the spoils!"

He pushed back onto his knees and slid down her body, his face zeroing in on her damp curls. He pushed her thighs farther apart and used his thumbs to spread her open. It made her sweat watching his eyes heat while he stared at her most intimate place.

"So beautiful, Calliope. I love your body." His next words were lost as he latched his mouth onto her exposed clit, sucking and nipping at the same time.

"Oh Goddess!"

The muscles in her legs contracted as she fought the urge to stretch them out and ride through the orgasm that was building fast.

A long finger slid inside her as his mouth continued its assault on her clit and she moaned. Nothing had ever felt as good as this. The sensations built quickly and she was getting closer and closer to the edge when he stopped.

She opened her mouth to protest, but he was too quick. He'd moved up her body again, and thrust inside her so deeply surely he was touching her heart. He stilled for a few seconds and she could feel the effort it took him to control his body. He wanted her pleasure and she loved him for that.

She lifted her head to kiss his shoulder and pulled her arms around his back, hugging his beautiful body closer to hers. Oeagus moved up to lean on his elbows and smiled as he slowly withdrew, then plunged in again, this time even farther than ever before. Her body clamped around his, never wanting him to leave.

Sighing, she closed her eyes. She wanted to stay this close to him forever.

"Look at me, Calliope," he said as he started a slow rhythm in and out.

His eyes never left hers as his hard cock worked its magic. As they both reached a mind-shattering climax, Calliope felt tears of joy trickle down her cheek. When he'd smiled, the fight was all over. He was definitely the victor and she never wanted to fight again.

Her heart clenched at the thought of never experiencing that again. She raised her head and kissed Gus on the mouth, a single tear trickling from her eye to his cheek.

His lips moved under hers as she would have pulled away. Sparks ignited between them when she deepened the kiss, energy flowing from her body into his. She shifted her hands to cup his face and she poured all of her love into him, feeling his life force return while the kiss continued.

"I guess this means our patient has woken up."

Callie smiled against Gus' lips. She reluctantly drew away, her eyes never leaving his beautiful face.

"It seems so, Doctor. My husband has returned to us."

Gus squeezed her hand. "You remember?"

She nodded, smiling so hard her face was aching. "I remember us."

He shouted at the ceiling, "Thank the gods!"

The doctor closed the curtains and stepped to the other side of the gurney. "Don't get yourself too excited, sir. I need to examine you to see if there are any lingering effects."

Gus smiled at Callie. "How can I not be excited when the first sight I lay my eyes on is perfection?"

The doctor smiled as he shined a torch into Gus' eyes one at a time. "I can certainly understand where you are coming from. Your wife is a beautiful woman."

"She certainly is. And she is mine."

Callie blushed, embarrassed by all the compliments. "Doctor, can I take my husband home now?"

"I think we should keep him until the morning at least. He still has a deep wound and he lost a lot of blood."

Gus threw off the sheet and lifted the hospital gown. "Check my wound. I feel well."

The doctor donned some blue gloves from a box on the wall before removing the dressing. "That's not possible!"

Callie looked at where the wound had been, seeing only a thin red line. "It mustn't have been as bad as you thought."

The doctor shook his head. "I swear, I stitched it up myself. I used two packets of sutures."

Gus grinned at him. "What can I say—I'm a fast healer."

The doctor headed out of the cubicle. "I've never seen anyone heal that fast. Stay here. I need to show one of my colleagues."

Eros walked past the doctor and entered, bringing Mardi with him. "I'm glad to see that love won out again. Good to see you back, my friend."

Gus sat up and swung his legs over the side of the gurney. "Quickly—we must leave. The doctor is questioning why I have healed so quickly."

Eros rolled his eyes. "These mortals can really be annoying sometimes."

Mardi's eyes widened. "Mortals?"

Callie glared at Eros. "Erie has a strange sense of humor sometimes. Do you have your car here, Mardi?"

"Yes I do, but is Gus well enough to leave?"

Gus smiled at Mardi, exuding power as he spoke. "I am more than ready, my dear. You will hurry to bring your car around and we will meet you out front."

Mardi nodded. "No worries. I'll see you at the patient pick-up zone."

Gus climbed out of the bed and dressed quickly before he and Eros transported them to behind a tree at the entrance to the hospital.

Callie's head spun when they got there, but she shook it off and peered out to make sure no one had seen them arrive. "I think it's all clear, boys, but just wait until I get you alone and I'll have a few words to say about using your powers on my friend."

Eros snorted. "You sound like your old self more and more with every passing moment."

"Don't think you're getting off scot free either, my dear cousin. You could have given me a bit more help when I asked for it."

"Hah! You had to find your power from within. If I'd transported us back to Mount Olympus, that might not have happened."

Gus covered her hands with his own, making her heart flutter with the joy of being with him again. "Please forgive me for convincing your friend to help us. It was the best option not to draw attention to us."

She smiled back at him. "I'll think about it. Just this once. I will not have my friends' minds controlled."

"Pftt," said Eros. "Like you've never done it before."

"That was before I came here and discovered what true friendship is. I won't be returning to my old ways."

"You weren't so bad, my beloved," said Gus as he turned her hands over and traced a finger over her palms.

"I was a spoiled child. I wanted my own way with everything."

"You never showed that side to me."

She laughed. "That's because you were spoiled enough for the two of us."

Eros coughed. "Ahem, I hate to break up your reunion, folks, but we have to get out of here."

Callie leaned forward and kissed Gus on the mouth before peering out from behind the tree. "There doesn't appear to be anyone searching for us out there."

Gus moved behind her. "There is Mardi's car. We should leave now in case they come looking for us."

Eros strode ahead of them shouting "shotgun" as they approached the car.

Callie glanced at Gus and they both laughed. "I think he spends way too much time here with the mortals."

"Yes, but if not for him doing just that, we would not have found you."

"Then it's a good thing. But let's not tell him that."

* * * *

Back at Serenity, Callie prepared to say goodbye to her friends. She knew the key to restoring her memories lay with her homeland, but she promised Mardi and Chris that she'd be back regularly to help with the shelter and her work there. It was too important not to. For now she and Gus had a special gift to leave them.

"Do you really mean that Serenity is now safe from intruders?"

"Yes, it's true. Only those invited in can walk through any of the doors."

"Wow. Just like vampires on *Buffy*."

Gus smiled at her. "Where do you think we got the idea from?"

Her eyes widened. "You're shitting me. Vampires don't exist." She frowned. "Do they?"

Callie laughed. "That's a story for another day, my friend. It's enough to handle the gods and goddesses thing for now."

"Perhaps you're right. Next time you visit you can tell me all about it."

"I will. I promise."

"I'm going to miss you so much," said Mardi as she hugged Callie one last time before they left. "You've taught me so much."

"That's what I was going to say to you," said Callie, returning the embrace. "I'm a much better person now. You showed me how wonderful it feels to help people. I'll never forget that."

"Ah, but you've taught me patience."

"She has?" laughed Eros. "That's not something I would ever have associated with Calliope."

Callie slapped him lightly on the back. "Shush, you. No giving up any more secrets about me."

Mardi grinned. "Too late. I'm learning more every minute."

"We should leave, my beloved."

Mardi threw her arms around his neck and kissed his cheek "Not until I get a hug from you too." She winked at him as she spoke. "And I would have driven you home from the hospital if you'd asked me."

Her husband blinked, appearing more nonplussed than she thought he could ever look. It seemed that these mortals had a thing or two to teach even a powerful warrior like Oeagus.

"My apologies—"

She shook her head. "None needed. I'm glad it all worked out for you. Now make sure you take good care of that wife of yours. She's one in a million."

Gus turned and pulled Callie against him, kissing the top of her head. "She is indeed, and I will try. Calliope is quite capable of caring for herself, but I will be keeping my eye on her all the same."

"After my recent experiences, I don't think I'll be objecting to your protection in a hurry, my love."

Gus smiled. "Knowing you, I expect that will wear off soon, but we can discuss that later. For now we must travel."

"Ready then?" asked Eros.

Callie smiled through tears as she waved one last time to her friends. "Yes. Let's go."

* * * *

"You have returned to us, my daughter."

Callie stood in front of her father and smiled with delight. "I am very happy to be back." She threw herself at him and hugged him tightly.

He hesitated for a few seconds before returning the hug. "I was worried the Titans would find you like they did your sister, Terpsichore."

"Corey? Is she okay?"

"I'm fine, sis," said a voice behind her.

She spun around and ran to her sister, throwing herself into her arms. "Thank the gods for that."

"And what's this I hear about you being with mortals in the place called Australia? So was I, but I never knew you were too."

"Really? Isn't it the most amazing place? Don't you just love those mortals?"

Corey beamed at her then turned to take the hand of a handsome blond stranger standing behind her. "I certainly do. Especially this one. This is James. He saved my life."

Callie wrapped her arms around him and kissed his cheek. "Thank you for saving my sister."

"It's a pleasure to meet you too," said James. "Corey has told me how close you two are. It's a great relief for her to know you're back where you belong."

"Okay, enough of this hug fest," said Eros, who entered the room accompanied by his beautiful wife Psyche. "How about telling everyone how I helped save you both."

"Silence!"

Everyone turned back to Zeus as he returned to his throne.

"I wish to hear of your intentions, Calliope. It seems that Terpsichore is so enamored with this mortal realm that she resides there most of the time. What say you of your plans?"

Callie turned to her sister. "Really?"

"Not now," she mouthed. "I'll tell you later."

"Calliope?" Her father sounded impatient.

"There is only one choice, Father. Oeagus is my husband. I must stay by his side."

Her father smiled. "Well—"

"However, we will be returning to the mortal realm often to visit," said Oeagus.

Her heart swelled. She knew that they'd already agreed on this, but she had been afraid of telling her father. That her big giant of a husband would take that worry away from her made her love him more.

"But what of your duties to your throne?"

Oeagus showed no fear and stood tall, leader to leader. "My armies are strong and my generals are capable. I can leave them from time to time. As have you with your own."

Zeus stood up, his imposing height no match for that of Oeagus, but the power he exuded more than made up for the difference. Callie took a step toward her husband, ready to intervene should her father wish him harm. Instead, she heard a bubble of laughter and watched as her father walked stepped forward and slapped her husband on the back.

"Excellent. I always knew I liked you. I respect a man who can stand up to me."

"I'm glad you approve, sir. However, be aware that I would have my wife happy no matter what you decide regarding her wishes. We will go back to our friends when we can, with or without your permission."

Zeus scowled and raised his hand. "What did you say?"

Callie stepped between them. "What he means, Father, is that he knows I'll go anyway, so he will accompany me to keep me safe."

His hand dropped back to his side, although the scowl stayed where it was. "Is that what you meant, Thracian?"

Callie grasped Gus' hand and squeezed it firmly. *Say yes. Say yes.*

He winked at her as he replied, "Of course, sir. Her safety is always my first consideration."

Her father sat back down again and they all started breathing.

"That's all right then. I think it's time for a banquet to celebrate your return." He clapped his hands and servants appeared carrying trays of delicacies and urns of wine, which they placed on a low table surrounded by plush velvet cushions. Zeus took a goblet from a servant and held it while it was being filled, his attention on Calliope. "In the morning we shall talk about where your other sisters might be. It strikes me as no coincidence that you both landed in the same world. Perhaps your other sisters are also there. This idea bears exploring."

Gus nodded. "This is an idea that also occurred to me, your greatness. I offer my services to assist in the search."

"Excellent."

"I'll help too," said Eros.

"Of course. We are already in your debt, Eros. Your knowledge of the mortal world has been invaluable. But for now, all of you sit and enjoy."

Callie and Gus sat with the other around the banquet, but neither was hungry for food. They listened in awe as Corey regaled them with how she'd been captured by Prometheus and taken to *The Underworld* before being rescued by James.

"Oh, my goddess. It seems we both had a big adventure. To think, we were both so close but didn't know it."

"I know," said Corey. "I thought of you often, though. I am so happy to have found you again."

She squeezed her sister's hand and smiled. It looked like the mortals had changed her as well. She turned her attention to the man by her sister's side. "So tell me, James. How did you and Corey meet?"

He laughed. "I was her solicitor."

"Solicitor?"

"That's lawyer in Aussie speak," said Corey.

"Oh," said Callie. "So why did she need a lawyer?"

"She got herself into a spot of bother," said James.

"What he means is, I was mistaken for a prostitute."

Callie laughed. "You're kidding!"

"No, she's not kidding," said James. "But it all turned out well enough."

"Absolutely," said Corey, her eyes shining as she and James shared a smile. "If not for that, we would never have met. And then who would have helped me out of *The Underworld*?"

"Indeed. It's wonderful to see you so in love. I would never have thought to see it happen."

"For a long time I've wanted what you two have. Now I have that, and I'm so glad you're back together."

Callie smiled at Gus, anxious to spend some time with him. "So am I."

Gus stood up, drawing her to her feet. "And on that note, my wife and I need to get further re-acquainted."

* * * *

Seconds later they were standing alone in their bedchamber in their home. Callie's eyes lit up as she whirled around, taking in her surroundings. "It's just as I remembered."

"I would not allow any changes. I wanted to keep it exactly as it was for your return, my love."

"Everything is not exactly the same, is it?"

He narrowed his eyes. "What do you mean? I will punish the servant who has not followed my orders."

She smirked, her lips twitching. "That's not what I'm talking about."

"Then what is different?"

"I seem to remember an argument shortly before I left."

His heart stopped. "I was stupid. I did not realize Pandora was trying to make trouble. Please forgive me, my beloved."

She walked to him, sliding her hands across his chest, staring up at him with those beautiful eyes. "I already have Oeagus, husband of my heart. Being away these past months has taught me to trust the feelings inside me, and I know you would never do anything to hurt me. It is I who should apologize to you for ever doubting you."

He threw his arms around her and held her close, feeling her firm body melt into his. "I will never again give you reason to, my love."

She smiled. "Oh, there will always be women throwing themselves at you, but in the future I will remind myself that I have your heart. I forgot that."

He laughed, flashing them to their soft bed. "I can think of a way we can show each other how sorry we are." Their clothes disappeared as he waved a hand in the air.

Calliope grinned up at him, sliding her arms around him. "I like the way you think."

He lowered his head and kissed the side of her neck. "It's time for you to stop thinking, and enjoy getting to know me again."

She shivered, turning her head to give him better access. "I think that can be arranged," she whispered. "I might need a lot of prompting, though. This could take a long time."

She felt him smile against her skin.

"That would be my plan," he said as he pulled her body tight against his.

She gasped. "Good plan." She reached up to his face and cupped his cheek.

He put his hand over hers, rubbing his face against it. He kissed her palm, her fingers, and her wrist before diverting his attention back to her neck. She gasped as his lips grazed a trail to her mouth.

He wrapped his arms around her and kissed her. Hard. Like striking a tender to a fire, her need for this man, her husband and lover, exploded and overwhelmed her. It was intense and bursting with emotion. She'd missed him, even when her memory had failed her. Her body was proving that now. The heat between them grew as their bodies moved together, touching each other with maximum exposure. He clasped her hands firmly and raised them above her head. She opened her eyes and gazed at him, watching every move he made, every touch of her skin, every caress.

He lifted her, pressing her body against the wall so that she straddled his hips. He kissed her again and she kissed him back, hungrily, sliding her hands back to his shoulders, clutching at him to keep upright as she rubbed her crotch against him, she tightened her legs around him, increasing the pressure against her heated sex.

He lifted her shirt and captured one breast and suckled before tugging lightly with his teeth. He squeezed her neglected nipple, twisting it gently. She moaned. She marveled at how he knew exactly where to touch her. How could she have forgotten this?

He moved on from her breasts and tickled his way across her skin with his hand until he reached between her legs, sliding a finger inside her. He added another, twisting and sliding them back and forth, scissoring his fingers and the small sting at being stretched.

"I need you," she whispered. "You are the man of my dreams."

"Not as much as I need you, my love, and the reality is so much better, don't you think?"

Her breathing was ragged and her muscles tensed.

"Oh, my goddess! Oeagus!" He ramped up the rhythm of his hand as he kissed her again.

.She spread her legs spread wider to him and he scraped his thumb over her clitoris as an orgasm burst free, sending her breathing into overdrive.

"Oooohhhh," she called out, unable to prevent a shout as he thrust joining their bodies.

Her muscles tightened around him, as he stilled and waited for her to catch her breath.

"Where did your clothes go?" She whispered.

He laughed. "I'm a demi-god remember. I wish them gone, and they are gone."

She smiled. "I forgot what a useful power that is."

"That's not the only useful power I have," he said as he withdrew and thrust inside her again.

She sighed happily. "Uh-huh".

"You are mine."

She groaned, gripping his shoulders and digging her fingers into his skin. "I am yours forever."

The pressure built again and she couldn't hold on for much longer. Gus sunk even deeper, managing to find a place inside her that set off her second explosive orgasm, tipping him over the edge until he came along with her.

When their breathing slowed down she caught his face in her hands and kissed him. "Thank the gods you found me. I didn't realize how much I missed this intimacy we share."

He stayed where he was, his body still firm within her and ready to go again. "I agree, my love. But I'm nowhere near finished getting intimate with you. Can you take some more?"

Her eyes twinkled. "Oh yes, my king. I certainly can."

He laughed as he proceeded to re-learn every inch of her body again.

And again.

About the Author

Maggie Mitchell lives in her dream place by the sea. Of course, sometimes she even gets the dreams written down in a story. Lucky for her she has a musician for a husband who understands the creative spirit.

In her other life she teaches undergraduate university nursing students and designs eLearning courses for health organizations.

Most days you'll find her out on her balcony enjoying a glass of Moscato or a cappuccino made on her beloved espresso machine.

Maggie Mitchell loves to hear from readers. You can find her contact information, website details and author profile page at http://www.totallybound.com.

Totally Bound Publishing